MYSTERY IN THE FARROWING BARN

To my grandchildren
for allowing me to tell on them.
Thank you Christina,
Sara,
Shawn,
and Steven McDade

To Sarah,

PIG OUT ON BOOKS!

Colene Copeland
1992

Contents

MYSTERY IN THE FARROWING BARN

By COLENE COPELAND
Illustrated By EDITH HARRISON

JORDAN VALLEY HERITAGE HOUSE

c.

MYSTERY IN THE FARROWING BARN

Jordan Valley Heritage House
43592 Hwy. 226
Stayton, Oregon 97383

Manufactured in the U.S.A.

Library of Congress Catalog
91-062326

ISBN: 0-939810-13-1 (Hardcover)
ISBN: 0-939810-14-x (Paperback)

First Edition

FORWARD

If you are familiar with the Priscilla series of books, you will enjoy being reunited with your old friends from the hog farrowing barn. If you are a newcomer to the pig world, you are about to embark on a journey to a place where animals talk to each other, and a few special ones can talk to humans, as well.

Here are some of the characters you will meet, as a teenaged cat, John Henry, is eager to solve the mystery of burglars in the farrowing barn, and everyone discovers the true spirit of Christmas.

MAMA and PAPA: The farm couple who operate a hog farrowing farm near Salem, Oregon.

THE KIDS: Grandchildren Christina, Sara, Shawn and Steven, who love to spend vacations with Mama and Papa and all the farm animals.

THE CAT FAMILY: T.C., a Tom Cat who had many adventures before he met Leeza, a thoroughbred Angora, and brought her back to the barn as his loving companion. Their kittens, John Henry, Slick, Emily and Angel are halfgrown, and as teenagers, cause a number of problems for their parents.

JIMMY and JENNY: Two children from the village who run away to escape a mean stepfather.

ROY McCOY: The abusive stepfather.

PRISCILLA, HOTSIE, MITZI and MABEL: Favorite sows and a poodle from years past. Mama and Papa loved them all, and when they died, each was buried in a Pet Cemetery in a beautiful part of the farm. Their graves were marked by boulders from the nearby river.

LITTLE PRISSY, PENNY, PATSY, ROSIE: Some of other special sows in the barn. Although Mama thought highly of all of them, Little Prissy, a daughter of Priscilla, was her current favorite. Priscilla and Mama had had a special gift of being able to talk with each other, and Little Prissy had inherited her mother's talent. The family did not talk about this strange gift because --well, outsiders wouldn't have believed it was possible.

Chapter 1.

A STRANGE CAT IN THE BARN

John Henry stood in the middle of the farrowing barn's hallway. The cat was center stage and engaged in one of his "doings". Since each of his "doings" was different, this one could be best described as mild, but silly.

Today, his neck was being put to the test. In a slow rhythmic motion John Henry's head turned from left to right, right to left, from left to right, back and forth, never stopping. The movement was as regular as the swinging of the pendulum on the big striking clock that sits on the mantel in the farmhouse.

When the animals in the barn began to stretch and yawn and to greet the new day, they woke to this strange scene. No one knew just how long John Henry had been engaged in this antic, but it was something new, so he was the center of attention.

T.C. (that's short for Tom Cat), stared at his son with unquestionable disapproval.

"Why?" T.C. asked himself. "After all, he's my son! How is it possible he turned out like this?"

Poor John Henry. He enjoyed himself. Being thought of as "strange" didn't bother him at all. But more than anything in the world he wanted his father to be proud of him. He longed for the day when his father would offer his approval, even if it was just a smidgen.

"Will that day ever come?" the kitten wondered sadly. "Likely not!"

Little Prissy smiled a knowing smile as she gazed sleepily at T.C., who hadn't taken his eyes off John Henry.

Prissy's pen felt roomier today. Just yesterday, thirteen out of the fourteen pigs in her last litter had been moved to the feeder barn. Pee Dee, the smallest pig, was left behind with her mother.

Once again, T.C. had become embarrassed by his son's odd behavior.

"John Henry, what is that you're doing?" he asked. "Why are you twisting your neck back and forth that way?"

John Henry showed no sign of stopping or even slowing down while he answered his father's question.

"I'm challenging my neck, Pop. I want to find out how long I can keep this up without my neck getting sore," he answered, seriously.

Prissy heard John Henry's answer and became concerned. "Or your head falls off!" she remarked.

Criticism didn't bother the kitten much, unless it came from his father. But this observation by Little Prissy was not necessarily appreciated.

"My head is not about to fall off, Prissy. You should try this sometime. It would do wonders for your triple chins!" he teased, hoping his comment would keep her quiet for a while.

Dozens of tiny pink, flat noses lined up behind the 2x4's of the hog pens. The pigs were curious. All of them tried to get a peek at what John Henry was doing this time. The pigs thought he was a really funny fellow.

The pigs were curious.

"Does it hurt yet?" little Pee Dee questioned.

"Of course not!" John Henry was glad to report.

Pee Dee had ideas of her own. "How can a cat be so serious about something so foolish?"she wondered.

As T.C. turned away, there was a disgusted look on his face. He leaped to the rafters above Prissy's pen and pretended to nap.

T.C. may have had some of them fooled, but not Prissy. Not for a minute! The little sow had known this fellow since she was a tiny pig. She knew that Tom Cat wasn't about to miss any of his son's silliness. No matter how skilled he was at pretending, Prissy was certain he was not napping.

In fact, Prissy had a good memory. She remembered her friend from days gone by. Looking up at T.C. and remembering brought a smile to her face.

"How he's changed, --the old faker," she thought. "Some of *his* stunts weren't so tame!"

"I wonder if he ever thinks about that?" Prissy mused.

Pee Dee glanced at her mother, then overhead at the Tom Cat.

"You wonder if he ever thinks about what?" Pee Dee asked.

Little Prissy motioned toward the cat above their heads and smiled at her daughter.

"See that cat up there, Pee Dee?"

"Yes, mother."

"That cat used to go flying around in these rafters overhead until my mother, Priscilla, and I thought he would surely fall and kill himself. Now look at him," Prissy grinned. "There he sits, all worked up over John Henry's stunts. Pee Dee, don't tell him I told you, but John Henry is a lot like his father, ---an awfully lot!"

Being ever so pleased that she had been entrusted to a secret, Pee Dee snorted a few squeaky giggles. Somehow, her mother's trust had caused her to feel differently, older perhaps, and special. After all, hadn't she been allowed to stay with her mother?

"My small size has its advantages," she thought.

"It's not just because you're smaller than the others," Prissy had told her. "It's because Mama, our owner, favors you. Your gentleness won her over, Pee Dee."

By now, the pigs had lost interest in watching John Henry do the same thing over and over. In fact, it became boring for everybody except John Henry, who was still looking to the left and to the right. He showed no sign of tiring.

One thing about it, John Henry was used to ridicule. The mocking and the belittling were constant. But did he care? No! Not a bit, ---as long as it wasn't his father doing the ridiculing. He took it all with an amazing sense of humor. His retorts to his ill treatment were playful and funny. So what if he wasn't like the rest of the cats? Who cared? Being different never bothered John Henry. After all, he took great pride in his special abilities and saw no reason to change.

"I'm a mismatch! My father said so." The cat knew he was supposed to take his father's words to heart and perhaps change his ways, but John Henry liked being called a mismatch. "It has a nice ring to it!" he laughed.

Now it sounds like John Henry might not have a friend in the world. Not true! There *was* someone, someone who believed in him, thought him adventuresome and exciting. That special someone was Penny, Little Prissy's daughter from a previous litter. Their friendship was unique. John Henry could always count on Penny. Much praise and approval came from this young sow. The cat's escapades delighted her. The only words to describe the way she felt about this fellow were sheer admiration. Occasionally, her friend needed a place to recuperate from one of his more strenuous capers. Penny's pen was the perfect place.

Her pen was next to Little Prissy's, so she had a clear view of the goings on. But today, like everyone else, she, too, had lost interest in this hum-drum exercise. Watching him steadily for a few minutes nearly put her to sleep. Now and then she glanced in the cat's direction to see if there was any change and to offer him words of encouragement. In the midst of all the sarcastic comments, Penny's kind words were truly appreciated.

"You'll set another record, John Henry," she said proudly. "Surely, no one has ever attempted to do what you are doing this time."

Penny's praise was sweeter than cream to the cat. He felt revitalized, ---so good in fact that he flexed his muscles and continued doing what he had been doing all day, but now he was doing it more vigorously. Left to right, right to left.

The one exception to John Henry's "not caring" feeling was the situation between himself and his father. The ambitious little cat truly loved and respected Tom Cat. Since he had been a tiny kitten, he had followed his pop around all over the farm and tried to be just like him.

John Henry was about half grown, sort of a teenage cat. More than once he had racked his brain trying to remember his first stunt, but he could not.

Actually, the first stunt took place on the tenth day of his life. The cat was born challenging his body. When a kitten is born, the eyes don't open for several days. John Henry hated it. He wanted to see. When his eyes finally did come open, he vowed he was going to keep them open. So, for as long as he could, he didn't blink. He felt that if he closed his eyes, they might just stay closed again. After he learned the truth about the eyes of a newborn kitten, he laughed at his mistake and began to plan another way to challenge his little body.

"You would think my father would be used to me by now," he had once confided in Penny. "So far, all I've heard from him is, 'Stop that, John Henry; you're going to kill yourself'; or 'Don't do that, son. It looks silly' and 'Quit that. You are embarrassing me' or 'I'm ashamed to be your father'."

Poor John Henry.

T.C. was a good cat. He had proved himself time and time again as a good father and friend. But for some reason, John Henry's way of life annoyed him. Perhaps he had forgotten what it was like to be young. There was a time, not too long ago, when the Tom Cat was considered to be a real crazy character. Quite a few females considered him to be the "cat's meow". Of course, that was before he fell madly in love with Leeza, John Henry's mother. But now he was a father and had taken up more serious, fatherly

ways. What a shame! The old T.C. was a lot more fun.

"It's hopeless," John Henry told himself. "He will never approve of anything I do, no matter what!" For now at least, there was Penny. Good old Penny. Thank goodness for her. Sadly, enough, as much as John Henry would like it, he didn't have Prissy's approval either.

"You shouldn't encourage him, Penny," Prissy told her daughter through the 2x4's dividing their pens. "Look what he's doing to his neck! That crazy fool cat is going to kill himself before he's had a

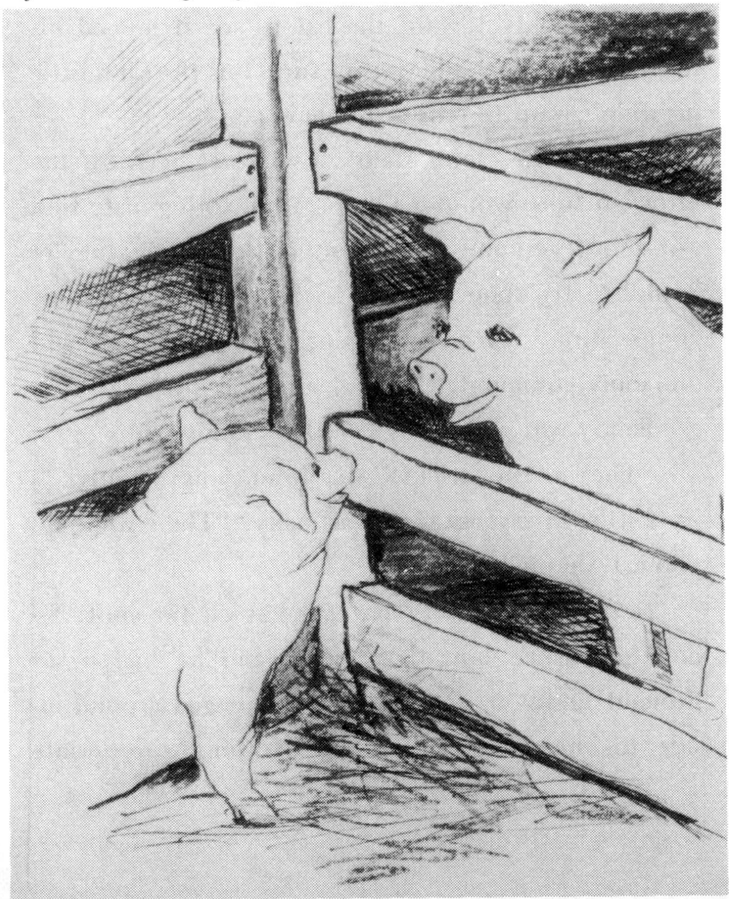

chance to grow up!"

"That's what you think, Prissy," John Henry grinned while looking from left to right, right to left. "You'll all be pea green with envy when I can do these things better than anyone else!"

"Anyone else who?" Pee Dee asked him. "Nobody does this silly stuff except you."

Several hogs laughed at what Pee Dee said. Their scornful laughter made the pig stop and think about what she had said. She felt ashamed.

"What if I've hurt his feelings?" she thought. She glanced quickly toward the cat to see if indeed his feelings were hurt. She wasn't sure. But the kind little pig didn't want to take any chances.

"Of course, John Henry, I've never been off the farm, so how would I know? When other cats find out about you and all the fun you are having, they're bound to try some of your tricks and give you some competition." To be really nice, she figured she'd add one more comment. "But I'm sure you'll win."

Penny was pleased by Pee Dee's kindness.

"They are not tricks!" was John Henry's reply.

Little Prissy asked sarcastically, "Then what do you call them?"

Her question really put the cat on the spot. No one had asked him that before and he had never thought about it. Quickly, he rummaged around inside his head for an answer. Nothing appropriate came to mind. If he was embarrassed or uncomfortable about Prissy's question, did he show it? Absolutely not!

Penny sprang to the rescue. "Why, mother, John Henry stays so busy all the time with his "doings" he hasn't had time to name them!"

When John Henry turned his head in her direction he shot Penny a grateful grin. But he continued looking from left to right and right to left.

Little Prissy suddenly remembered a big word and was proud of herself. "Decathlon!" she exclaimed with pleasure and surprise.

"What?" Pee Dee had never heard such a word. "Did you sneeze, mother?"

Prissy chuckled at that. Then before you could say "cold corn flakes", Tom Cat jumped from the rafters, landing ker-wham on the top boards of her pen.

"Porker, yes! Decathlon!" T.C. had not called Little Prissy by her nickname for quite a spell. "I remember too! Priscilla told us about watching the Olympics on television when she lived in the farm house." The cat was excited about remembering. He showed white, sharp teeth when he talked.

"A contest between athletes, right?" Prissy asked T.C.

"One person had to be skilled in several events, like running, jumping, swimming and so on," he proudly informed her.

"I'm good at lots of things," John Henry thought as he listened to his father. "Why can't he get excited about my events?"

Tom Cat and Prissy became so engrossed in their mulling over the interesting life Priscilla had lived in the house that they forgot all about the problem at hand, which was to give a name to John Henry's "doings".

The young cat was pretty aggravated at both of them. "That decathlon business sounds like human stuff to me! Have you noticed lately? I'm a cat!"

"Then why don't you call your "doings" the "de-CAT-lon?" Penny giggled noisily at her own suggestion.

Whether or not John Henry liked the idea, one could not tell.

Suddenly, it occurred to T.C. he might have sent the wrong signals to his son. Encouraging John Henry in any way to pursue this life of foolishness, was not intended. Quickly, he sprang to his perch in the rafters and faked disinterest.

"Scrud", John Henry muttered quietly. "Just when I thought he might be showing a little interest in me, up he goes, to escape. Well, double scrud and phooey on my pop!"

Chapter 2.

A PAIN IN THE NECK

About noon, T.C.'s second son Slick, loped cautiously through the front door of the farrowing barn. Even though John Henry wore a golden coat, both of them looked a lot like their father. But that's where the likeness ended. "Two peas in a pod", they were not! No two brothers were less alike.

Slick kept his distance from his brother. He could not stand John Henry. But here they stood, face to face. Every other time John Henry turned his head, he was face to face with his brother. Slick took a wide berth around the cat. For a moment he stopped and stared in downright disbelief at this kind of tomfoolery. He made no effort to hide his feelings. Slick saw his brother as an absolutely irresponsible nuisance, as well as an annoying foe. For the moment at least, he felt safe to be near his brother. John Henry

Slick grooming

was too busy to be bothered by Slick.

Slick jogged on by. About twenty feet down the hallway he leaped up on the lid of a feed barrel and began to groom himself. Slick was always grooming himself. That's why Papa named him Slick in the first place. Sometimes Mama called him Tubby. She told Papa she thought God made a mistake.

"I don't know why Slick wasn't born a pig. He eats like one!" True enough. "I can't put enough food outside to fill him up," Mama complained. "Sometimes I feel like putting a salt shaker in his paw and telling him to go on out to the back yard and graze." she laughed.

John Henry worked hard at earning the opinion his brother had of him. The most enjoyable times in his life had come from tormenting his brother.

Slick took great pride in keeping himself spotlessly groomed. But when John Henry was around, Slick worried, with good reason.

John Henry would hide around corners out of the sight of his unsuspecting brother. Dry and murky spots were best. When he sighted Slick, all spruced up, clean as a whistle, John Henry would wait patiently until Slick was within range. Then he would spin around, his back to his brother and with all four feet, as fast as a super-powered cat can claw the ground, let fly with dirt and dust, ---all over his brother's clean fur.

Startled always, Slick would shake himself, swear and screech like a panther, all the while running for cover. Meanwhile, John Henry held his stomach and rolled with laughter in the dirt! As soon as one attack was over, John Henry started planning a new one. With his mischievous nature, he could hardly wait for his next opportunity. And there would be one - soon!

The pleasure John Henry got out of getting his brother dirty was purely sinful, but ---it was so much fun!

His greatest satisfaction came the day he caught Slick sitting quietly in the cow pasture. His brother looked so peaceful, just sitting there with his tail wrapped around himself, waiting. He had seen a fat mouse run into a hole, and it was just a matter of time. Slick licked his lips in anticipation.

John Henry sneaked up behind his brother and yelled!

"Mouse! Mouse!"

Turning quickly, Slick faced his brother.

John Henry, feet planted firmly in a pile of dry cow manure, began to scratch! You never saw a cat's feet move faster. It was like watching the spinning spokes on a fast moving bicycle. All sizes of chunks of the smelly stuff flew into Slick's face and covered his immaculately clean fur. The surprise caught the cat with his mouth wide open. In went some of the yucky pieces. All Slick wanted to do was get away from this conniving hellion. He leaped wildly into the air before high-tailing it across the pasture.

John Henry couldn't help himself. He laughed until his sides hurt. Later, everytime he thought about it, he started laughing all over again.

Is it any wonder that Slick kept his distance from his brother? John Henry had been warned by his father!

"One day your brother will get enough of your pranks. And when he does, he'll get even with you." John Henry didn't think so.

All these fun thoughts about his brother had given him something to occupy his mind while he

John Henry, feet planted firmly in a pile of dry cow manure, began to scratch!

looked from side to side.

Long after the hogs had their evening meal, long after Papa and Mama finished their evening chores, and long after everything of importance that day had happened, John Henry began showing signs of tiring.

Then "clunk", it happened. The "doing" was done. John Henry's neck was stuck in left position! It was parked! He tried to jerk it loose! That hurt! He spun around and scratched the floor. The sound that came out of the kitten's mouth was unbelievable! He screeched an ear piercing, unnerving wail. But nothing changed! His neck stayed parked in left.

John Henry's neck was stuck in left position!

The racket rattled the barn! Every animal in the barn rose up to check out the fuss.

An angry old sow whose rest had been interrupted sprang to her feet.

"What's the matter with you, cat? If I had a bucket, I'd throw it at you!"

John Henry did not answer the sow. He was too stunned to function properly.

Little Pee Dee peeked through the 2x4's. "Did you hurt yourself, John Henry?" she asked slowly, yawning and rubbing her little eyes.

No answer.

Tom Cat woke up and looked down from his perch. Although the concern he felt for his son was genuine enough, he offered no words of sympathy. Nor did he make any attempt to help him or go near him.

Prissy watched John Henry's predicament. It was an extremely frightful situation the cat had gotten himself into. With his head all locked to one side, the cat looked painfully funny. Suddenly, without any warning, Prissy began to laugh, which immediately embarrassed her. It was not like her to laugh at someone helpless and suffering. She tried to stop, but she could not! First it was a snicker. She tried to hide it. But then it sort of exploded like the burst of a bomb. The laughter swelled until the sow's large frame shook! The harder she tried to stop laughing, the more violent her laughter became.

Poor John Henry! Little Prissy had infected everyone. Now, all of them gawked and snickered as the poor cat just stood there. He did look funny, but the cat didn't think it was very amusing. It hurt! How humiliating to have this happen in front of his father. With the barn dimly lighted, plus the condition of his neck, he was not able to look upward to see his father's face. He didn't give two hoots about the others; not even Prissy's laughter ruffled him.

"Who cares about that?" he told himself. For indeed he did not care.

Slick had taken off toward the back of the barn the moment the ruckus commenced. Even though he had been sleeping peacefully in the office by the heater and was out of sight, he knew if he laughed, he'd be heard. And John Henry would get even, somehow.

To make matters worse, John Henry was forced to shuffle along sideways to escape through the front door. He really didn't care how he did it, he just wanted to get out.

Once outside, he hid himself under a large Oregon juniper bush. Crumpled there on the ground, the cat began to cry. Not just because of the pain, but rather because he was sure he heard his father laugh. John Henry hoped with all his heart that he was mistaken.

Would John Henry ever earn his father's approval?

Chapter 3.

HOME REMEDIES

For the past couple of weeks the weather had been unusually pleasant, the kind that makes one think about planting a garden or going fishing. But it was the tenth of December, two weeks before Christmas. And according to Jim Bosley, Papa's favorite and trusted weatherman, things were about to change. By evening, there was a crisp bite to the air.

But no matter. Cold or hot, flood or tornado, when it's a sow's time to have her babies, have them she will. Tonight it was Penny's turn and all went well. By midnight, ten healthy, frisky little pigs had nursed their mother and now slept soundly under the heat lamp in the corner creep.

As usual, Papa and Mama had been on hand the entire time. Now, before going to the house, they stopped by the office at the front of the farrowing barn. At one time the office had been a hog pen. A few years ago Papa had a local carpenter, Tom Moore, convert it into an enclosed multi-purpose room. It was handy.

In it was a small desk where Papa kept the records of all the sows, a telephone, a small refrigerator, a small table and chairs, two narrow cots and two small stoves. After all, it was a "small" room. Tonight the little wood burning stove was getting a rest in the corner. But the little electric heater hummed as it warmed the room.

Papa poured them each a cup of hot chocolate from a thermos bottle. He spilled a few drops on the table and wiped it up with his glove.

A cat scratched on the office door. It was not the strong, demanding and impatient scratch they'd gotten used to, but rather a weak, pawing sound, ---followed by faint meowing.

"What in the world is that?" Mama hurried to the door.

There stood John Henry. His condition had not changed or improved. In order to see where he was going, he walked at an angle. It was like a car clipping down the road with a busted frame. Somehow he managed to thrust himself through the open door. For a moment he just stood there, meowing, clearly in great pain. Staggering clumsily ahead, he rammed his twisted head into the woodbox. He let out a tormented groan. His voice was hoarse and raspy.

"Poor, pitiful kitten," Papa said, feeling sorry for the suffering animal.

Out of desperation, John Henry had come to them for help. He had voiced his misery for so long that his throat was sore. At the moment, it felt as though he had swallowed a fire cracker.

"I can't stand to see the poor thing suffer," Mama said. "But I don't have the nerve to call the vet at this hour of the night!"

Papa laughed at the thought of calling Mike in the middle of the night to attend a cat with a sore neck!

When John Henry tried to jump on Papa's lap, the sad little tabby fell to one side. With both hands opened wide, Papa lifted the cat gently to his arms.

After rummaging around for a few seconds in the first aid box, Mama found the liniment.

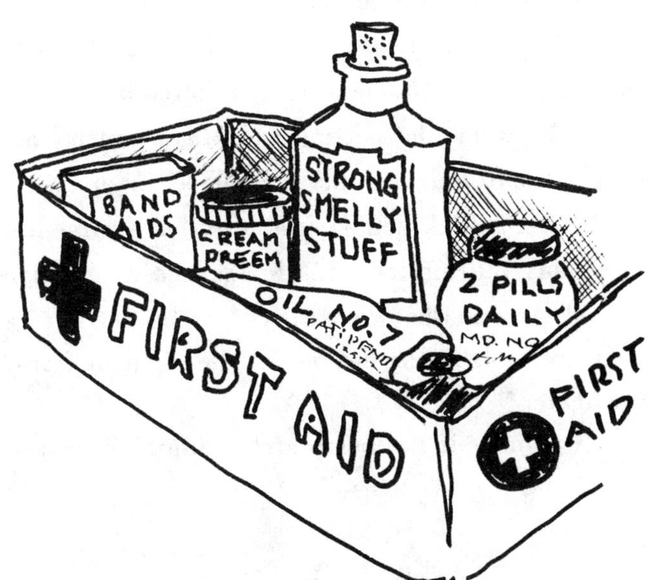

"Good idea," Papa agreed. He put on a pair of leather gloves. "I'll hold him, you rub it on."

"I'm glad you're going to hold him!" Mama grinned as she uncorked a bottle of strong smelly stuff and began dabbing it on the cat's neck. The few seconds it took to saturate the affected area seemed more like an eternity.

John Henry growled, hissed, clawed and tried to escape. He wanted help, but he was frightened and tormented.

Putting on those leather gloves turned out to be a smart move. However, they provided no protection for Papa's legs. For his age, John Henry was quite strong and muscular. He struggled wildly to free himself! Suddenly, he freed a hind leg. Papa's knee took a painful clawing. It hurt like the dickens. But there was no use complaining. Who could hear him anyway over John Henry's loud cries?

When the medicating ordeal was over, Papa held the cat firmly with one hand and petted him with the other. Between the petting and Mama putting away that bottle of liniment, the cat calmed down a little.

"I don't think you'll get him settled down enough to do any purring tonight," Mama said as she placed an old shirt in the wood box. "If the cat is smart, he'll lay in here for the rest of the night in front of the heater."

"I wonder if the burro kicked him?" Papa asked.

"Good golly!" the cat thought. "I was doing so well, too, until my neck parked itself."

Mama was surprised at Papa. "You think Piston did this? He wouldn't! He's been a perfect angel. Remember how he used to run off all the time when the Greystones owned him?"

"That burro got his belly full of running around when that old rip from the carnival stole him."

"I still can't bear thinking about it," Mama replied sadly. "How anyone could mistreat an animal like that old Rossi mistreated Piston is more than I can understand. I'm so proud of the grandchildren for rescuing Piston."

Although Papa hadn't noticed John Henry's neck challenge today, he had seen the cat walking around under Piston's feet one day. "Kinda crazy like," he had said, "weaving in and out, he was, ---never stopping." It didn't seem to bother the burro and the cat appeared to be having a good time, so Papa left them alone.

Of course, what Papa had witnessed was one of the cat's "doings". That day, he just wanted to see how long he could stay under Piston without getting stepped on. Wherever the burro walked, so did the cat, staying between all four legs. Finally, the burro laid down in the pasture. That ended the "doings". John Henry got away without a scratch.

Papa and Mama took a last look at Penny's family

before going to the house.

The wood box was full of John Henry. The heat and the liniment were doing the job. The cat was asleep, probably dreaming of wonderful ways to challenge his body.

What will he bust up next?

Chapter 4.

GETTING TO KNOW THE CAT FAMILY

Papa and Mama were not exactly ready for what they found when they went back to check on Penny one more time before going to the house. The surprise didn't involve the little sow or her new family. With them, all was perfectly normal. Her pigs had come out of the creep again to nurse. Most of them were asleep by their mother.

The news was next door. Patsy, Penny's sister was in labor. Already three newborns were running around in the pen, ---looking cute and cuddly.

"Couldn't you wait one more day, honey, like you were supposed to?" Mama asked as she patted the sow's side.

"No, she couldn't," Papa grinned. "Penny has pigs, Patsy wants some too! Right, girl?"

Somehow, Papa and Mama found the needed strength to stay and assist Patsy. About 2:30 in the morning, the fifth pig was born, a white little thing, unusually long. Papa was genuinely pleased. The last white hog in this line was Mabel, a Landrace. But Mabel never gave birth to a white pig. Priscilla was her daughter. She was red with a white belt and legs. Priscilla's Little Prissy was rusty red. All the others were red and white. Oddly enough, this white baby pig looked like a purebred Landrace, although it was not.

When Mama returned from the office with a box of birthing supplies, she, too, spotted the new white miracle. She gazed in awe at the tiny thing. A long tear made its way down her cheek.

"Oh, Mabel, I wish you could have lived to see this," Mama said to herself. She picked up the pig to get a better look. Yes, it was a girl!

Soon, Patsy had given birth to eleven pigs. One weak little fellow was born dead. Papa wrapped it in paper towels, put it in a bucket and covered it with straw. Come morning, they would bury it back in the timber, in the pet cemetery, and by all means, it would be buried next to Mabel.

Arley Willett was scheduled to show up at 7 A.M. to help with some of the work. Papa left a note on the office door. It read, "It is 4:30 A.M. You'll notice there are twenty more pigs. See you about nine, maybe ten". Papa drew a little picture of a man with his eyes shut.

The rest of the cat family had gone into the office

Papa's note.

through the pet door. Tom Cat, Leeza, Slick and the two girls, Emily and Angel, joined the ailing John Henry.

Slick figured he'd be safe, for now.

When she saw John Henry's dilemma, Leeza began the motherly task of licking at the affected neck. But one taste of that foul, smelly liniment put a stop to that! She switched her attention to cleaning his paws.

There were no words spoken. Not one. No motherly advice nor fatherly opinions for John Henry. Slick dared not tease his brother. He spent his time grooming or sleeping. Though they said nothing, John Henry was aware of the love and compassion from his sisters. Angel said it all with her very expressive eyes. Emily helped her mother with her brother's grooming. Unlike his brother, John Henry always needed grooming.

The girls were beautiful white angoras like their mother. Emily was shy and gullible."Gullible" should have been Emily's middle name. She would believe anything. Leeza kept hoping that the kitten would wise up.

John Henry once told Emily that spaghetti was made out of watermelon. She believed him.

Angel had a different kind of problem. Anything a cat could fear was on her list of "things to be afraid of". Number one on her list was mice! Strange indeed for a cat. Her fear was genuine. She was even afraid of the young pink ones. Her fear caused her parents great concern. Kill a mouse and lay it in front of her and she would eat it, but let a live one cross her path and she made tracks in the opposite direction. Of course, she wouldn't starve. Cat food was always available. Everyday fresh food was put out by the office door and also on the back porch of the farm house. The wild cats from the timber usually polished that off, at night.

"Someday I'll have to do something about Angel's fear of mice," T.C. told Leeza. "After all, she's a cat! Every farm cat is obligated to do its part in keeping down the rodent population. Rodents carry disease! Fewer mice and rats mean a cleaner barn and healthier hogs. And, that's the name of that tune." Tom Cat was quoting some of the things he had heard Papa say. "A cat must pay its own way!" Very soon

T.C. would take his daughter in hand. He would think of something.

The rest of the night passed quickly. By morning a gentle rain pattered quietly on the roof of the barn.

When Arley arrived, he read Papa's note. He wondered if one sow had given birth to twenty pigs! The answer was not long in coming. He put feed pellets in each pen and was greeted happily by the two sows and their babies. Penny and Patsy were both proud to show off their new families, ten pigs each. Little Prissy and her daughter chatted happily. Prissy was pleased that Pee Dee had been allowed to remain with her.

When the cat family woke up, one was missing.

"John Henry is not here, mother," Emily said sweetly."Do you suppose he has hurt himself again?"

"Don't worry about your brother, Emily. Somehow he manages to live inspite of his strange behavior," Leeza answered.

Slick was ready for his gullible sister.

"The last time I saw John Henry he had screwed his head clean off, tied it to his tail and was dragging it on the ground." Slick could see that Emily was believing everything he said. Her eyes grew large and her mouth dropped open. Seeing this, Slick determined he'd make his yarn a little more gruesome, so he added, "Then he dragged it through the blood of this dead horse. The one that was half eaten by a bear in the night."

Emily gasped! Thinking the worst had happened to her brother, the cat began to wail.

"Don't believe him, Emily. It is not true," Leeza said, trying to console her innocent little daughter.

T.C. wasn't quite so calm, In an attempt to teach Slick a lesson, he struck him hard across the head with his right front paw. "Whack!" The surprised cat went sprawling across the office floor. The girls loved it! He had it coming! Slick sprang to his feet and dived out the pet door.

Meanwhile, John Henry, who had nearly recovered, visited Penny and her pigs. The sow was anxious to know if the cat still had a neck that worked properly. With exception of a minor twinge of pain now and then, the cat had forgotten all about yesterday's misery. He had completely put it out of his mind. The fact is, John Henry never dwelled on the past, or what had been; rather he concerned himself with today. How could he best spend the day? How could he improve himself? What would this new day have to offer him?

Those who still had yesterday on their minds, those who wanted to scoff and tease about his misery and make fools of themselves were of no interest to John Henry.

"Ask me if I care," he said to Penny. Penny did not ask. She already knew the answer.

When John Henry was satisfied that all was well with Penny, he began to think and to make plans. Penny knew from past experiences that John Henry would not wait to recover completely from one "doings" before jumping headlong into a new one.

While John Henry cooked up new plans in his head, he took time to greet each of Penny's children. One sassy little fellow commenced rooting at the cat. Why? Because pigs naturally root at everything. They come that way! But this pig jarred John Henry, ---a little too much. The cat's neck was almost, but not quite straight. The pig's hard little nose had forced the cat to jerk his neck to the right. It did smart.

"Good-bye, pigs!" he shouted, and he was gone. And, one wonders, to do what?

Chapter 5.

STORMY WEATHER

While Arley Willett babysat the pigs, Papa and Mama went to Salem to finish the Christmas shopping. Their list was long, but it was Tuesday, the weather was wet and miserable, the wind was blowing, and there were very few shoppers brave enough to come out.

"People with good sense stayed at home by the fire today," Papa observed.

"We'll finish up in the mall, where it's dry," Mama replied. "We can have lunch there, too."

The two of them had a very pleasant day away from the farm. Several times boxes and packages had to be rearranged in the station wagon to make room. They especially enjoyed all the Christmas decorations and the music. Papa bought a couple of new albums of carols. One was new arrangements of old favorites. He was eager to put it on the stereo.

Several times boxes and packages had to be rearranged in the station wagon to make room.

Before heading back to the farm, they stopped by their daughter Deana's house. The family had just gotten home with a freshly cut Christmas tree. Strings of lights and ornaments were all over the floor. Steven tried to see himself in a large, silver ornament. He smiled and made faces. Christina and Sara were busy untangling the strings of lights. Shawn was on the phone ordering pizza.

"Say you'll stay, Grandma, and I'll order two large instead of two medium," Shawn hollered from the kitchen.

"Pizza? We'll stay!" their grandfather answered. "I'll bring in some pop. I bought it for you kids anyway. You might as well drink it here as at the farm."

The girls asked about their favorite hogs, Thunder and Crackerbelle, and about the new pigs. But they saved the most important question for last. How much of their Christmas holiday were they to get to spend on the farm?

"I hear there's a big storm coming," Deana told them. "You might get snowbound out there. Maybe you wouldn't be able to get back to school."

"Yeah!" Steven shouted. "Let it snow! No school! I'll build a snowman, ---lots of them." Steven was seven.

"And put Grandpa's hats on them," Shawn added.

"And Grandma's long red apron," Sara laughed,

remembering the snow family they built last year on the farm.

"Maybe we should take all of you home with us now,before the storm hits. Then let the storm come!" Mama told them.

"They'd like that all right," Deana smiled at the kids, "But there are a few more days of school."

"Oh Mom! You're no fun," Sara twisted her face into a frown. Then she shook the last tangle from a string of lights. It was Christina's job to put them on the tree.

The family had a tradition about the trimming of the tree. Each member of the family had a task to perform. Deana held on to Steven's leg as he stood on the top rung of the ladder to put the star in place, at the very top. He was grinning as he pretended to shake the ladder, to scare his mom.

The pizza arrived. The family sat around the tree to enjoy the food among the mess of boxes on the floor.

"Isn't Christmas pretty?" Steven declared.

Christina put her arm around him and gave him a kiss.

"Yes, Darling," she told him, "and so are you, pizza face and all."

The kids would sleep on the floor in the living room that night. It was their way to welcome Christmas. They did it every year.

It was about a 45 minute drive back to the farm. The temperature was still dropping, making the evening weather even more miserable than the day's had been.

Papa turned on the car radio trying to hear a weather report.

"I'm not sure I want to hear it," Mama told him. "I wish it could stay nice for Christmas."

"A lot of folks prefer a white Christmas," Papa reminded her.

"Not me!" Mama was serious. "I prefer clear skies and safe roads."

As soon as the car was unloaded, Papa changed his clothes and walked the well-beaten path to the barn. It was a cold, wet walk. About half way across the orchard, he wished he had driven the old pickup.

Arley was still there, working on an overhead heater fan.

"Got trouble?" Papa asked.

"Not yet. I remembered this fan was squeekin' the last time we had it runnin'. So I thought I'd better oil it a little. Have you heard the latest weather report?" he asked.

"No. I had the car radio on, but just as the weatherman came on we drove under the power lines. All I got was static!" Papa laughed.

"Freezin' rains a comin'! Temperatures in the 20's," Arley reported. "That's why I'm oilin' up this ol' fan."

"And I appreciate it," Papa told him.

Before Arley left for home, he pointed to a pile of dead mice in the hallway, outside Penny's gate.

"That cat, John Henry, he's been killin' mice and pilin' 'em up right there, all day. Why do you suppose he's doin' that?"

Little Prissy and Penny were listening to Arley. They exchanged knowing glances. It pleased them to know something the humans didn't. John Henry had set another record, "Mice caught and killed, but not eaten, 27"! The sows had last seen the cat about half an hour ago. He was drenched to the bone. Penny had asked him to come in and dry off, but he was hungry. The cat had seen so many mice that day he didn't care to eat one. He'd head down to the farm house where there was always dry cat food on the back porch. Maybe after supper they would see John Henry again, maybe not.

Neither Papa nor Arley could guess how much that heater fan was going to be needed. They could not have guessed just how cruel nature intended to treat them. For the next three days a freezing rain fell, seldom letting up. Those three days, December 13, 14, and 15 were days they'd remember. For the first 30 hours of that time, there was no electricity. Heavy ice weighed down the power lines. The line snapped! Off went the power!

The men from the power company worked day and night trying to restore service. When they were working near the farm, Papa took them out a thermos of something hot to drink. They appreciated his thoughtfulness.

Papa was just about ready to turn off the bedroom light and jump into bed when the power failed, the lights flickered, and the room was in darkness.

"Oh no! The current's off." He scrambled around in the dark to get dressed. Mama was asleep, but when Papa stubbed his toe on the metal leg of the bed and began to dance around and swear a little, Mama woke up.

"What's wrong with you?" she asked.

"The power went off," he answered. He was hopping around on one leg, holding his sore-toed foot in his hands.

A candle and matches were always in readiness on Mama's side of the bed. She lit the candle and also the kerosene lamp in the hallway. Thank goodness, they didn't depend upon electric heat. The big wood heating stove downstairs in the family room kept the entire house nice and warm. But out in the barn there would be no heat. The heat lamps were off.

Papa bundled up quickly and went slip-sliding across the icy ground in the orchard. Several years ago he had purchased a generator for times like this for emergency power.

In the darkness, Papa stubbed his toe.

The pigs could survive the cold by getting in under the straw with their mother. But could they survive their mother? The sow might accidently lay on one or two of them. The heat lamps in the creeps were much safer and more comfortable.

Except for Papa's big flashlight, the barn was dark. The sows were concerned and were calling to their pigs. But in a matter of minutes, the generator was running and so were the heaters, the lights and

Christmas has finally returned.

best of all, the heat lamps. Papa walked down the hallway to make sure everything was okay.

By being prepared, Papa and Mama had managed to get by without electricity for those 30 hours. What they missed most were the lights on the Christmas tree. When the power company finally restored service and the tree lights were shining brightly again, Papa announced, "Well, Christmas has finally returned."

The generator was used for the barn only. However, had the power outage lasted much longer, a small generator would have been powered up for the house, mainly to keep the food in the freezers frozen.

Now, Christmas was less than two weeks away. Ever since he could remember, Papa had loved Christmas music. When he couldn't locate some on the radio, he'd pile on a stack of records. The little radio in the office was getting a constant workout of dial twisting, to find carols.

The animals enjoyed the music. Pee Dee tried to sing. She was sure she could if she practiced.

It was hard to tell if John Henry liked the music. Today hs looked terrible. He refused food, and hid under the barn when Mama told him she was going to take him to see the vet. This time he had challenged his stomach. No food! Slick thought *that* was the dumbest thing he had ever heard.

"If that cat doesn't take to eatin' somethin', he's gonna die!" Arley told Papa.

T.C.'s family overheard Arley's comment. Angel cried when she heard the news.

Tom Cat wondered if this time his son had gone too far. Would John Henry really starve himself to death?

Angel cried!

Chapter 6.

WHERE ARE THE CHILDREN

Regardless of the weather, on the farm something always needed fixing. Today was no different than any other. Papa was out by the road repairing a broken hinge on the big metal gate. It was a cold job.

The mailman came. He pulled over sufficiently to reach the mailbox, rolled down the window and said hello to Papa.

"Wouldn't want your job, Will. How do you manage on these slick roads?" Papa asked.

"Practice neighbor, practice," Will grinned. "I've got to deliver this mail, just like you have to get out here in the cold to take care of your livestock. This weather has been the pits! Wouldn't you agree?"

Papa agreed. It was nice to have someone to visit with for a little while. The mailman always knew everything that was going on. Papa and Mama hadn't been off the place for a few days and hadn't heard any local news. Some of the news Papa heard from Will was not good, not good at all.

That evening at the supper table over good, hot, homemade potato soup, Papa shared some of the local gossip. The hot soup was a great way to top off a cold miserable day.

"Mary Parker's children are missing!"

"Missing?" Mama didn't like the sound of that. "How can that be? Are you sure? Did they run away, or did somebody run off with them?"

"Don't know. Will said that Mary is back in Iowa. Her brother is hurt bad, the younger one who rides in rodeos. Will said the fellow got thrown off a bull, then the cussed animal spun around and rammed a nine inch horn through his chest. He's pretty bad off; ---might not make it." Even with all that bad news, Papa went for his second helping of the soup and another hot roll. "She left the children ---"

Mama interrupted. "There's two of them, a boy and a girl."

"Yes, ---there's a boy and a girl. The boy is older, eight or nine, maybe. Mary left them behind with this new fellow she's married to."

"I've heard about him. Roy McCoy. I remember his name because it rhymed," she laughed. "So, Mary's not a Parker anymore."

"With Mary out of town, this Roy Boy's been

spending a lot of time at Bessie's." Bessie's was a local bar.

Mama didn't like hearing that. "Who takes care of the children?"

"Will says Roy takes them along in his pickup truck. Said he left them sitting out in front of Bessie's. Nobody knew they were out there until Roy Boy came runnin' back into the place hollering, 'They've gone! The kids are gone!' Seems like everybody's been lookin' for the kids but they've sure enough dropped out of sight."

"When did this happen?" Mama asked.

"Saturday night. That's four days ago. Hard telling if somebody took 'em, or they just plain ran away from ol' Roy. Nobody knows how to get in touch with Mary, except for Roy Boy, and I'll bet he's afraid what will happen when she finds out."

"I don't blame him for being afraid," Mama quipped, knowing how she would feel if someone mistreated one of her kids. "I'll bet those two children, if they did run away, went to their grandparents' place over in Cottonwood."

"How would they get there?" Papa asked.

"Kids are smarter than you think. There's a lot of good people in Thomas Creek. Almost anyone would have taken them over there. Not only would they take the kids to their grandparents, they'd never tell a soul." Mama thought about it for a minute. "I would have taken them, gladly. They'd be safe then until their mother got back." She laughed. "In fact, I wish I'd been the one that took them."

"Can you imagine that fellow leavin' those children out in his pickup truck on such a cold night?" Papa asked.

"No, I can't," Mama answered. "I don't think I like him very much. I remember how cold it was Saturday night!"

As the two of them cleaned up the supper dishes, they thought about the children and wished there was something they could do.

The worst part of the storm passed. During the day, the temperature had gotten up to 35 degrees. The sun even came out for a few minutes. But before dark, the thermometer dropped again and with it came the cold, bone chilling, miserable rain.

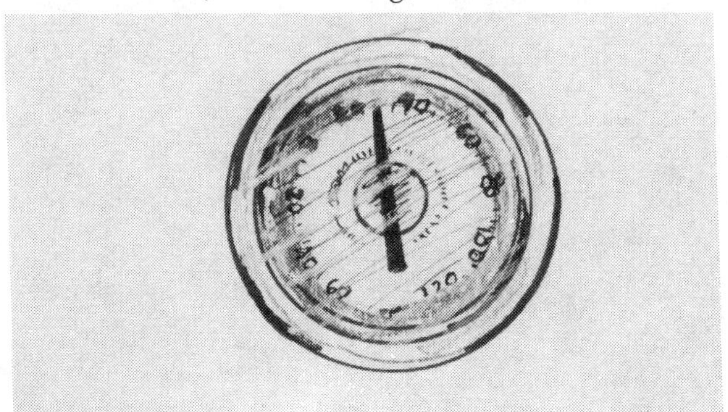

Nevertheless Papa deemed it necessary to make one last trip to the barn.

"Can't take chances with my hogs," he said.

Papa had a secret. He had put off telling it to Mama just about as long as he could. For the past few nights someone had been sneaking into the barn, taking things from the office. Not money. None was kept there. It was mainly food. Someone had been taking a little food and a few cans of pop, every night. They even took the two blankets that were kept in the office for those cold nights when pigs were being born.

Tonight, as Papa drew near the front door of the barn a strange feeling overtook him. He felt he was being watched. He looked around and saw no one.

"Should I be afraid?" Papa asked himself.

Once he was inside the building, he felt more comfortable; he also felt a little foolish.

But it still made him wonder. Was someone out there?

Chapter 7.

LAST SATURDAY NIGHT

Roy McCoy was already half-drunk when he pulled up in front of Bessie's Bar. He lit a cigarette and let it flop up and down on his lips as he barked off a full set of orders to his step-children.

"Stay out here! Don't get out of this truck," he snapped. With each command his fist came down hard on the steering wheel. "Eat that sack of potato chips. When I get through in here, I'll take you some-place and buy you a hamburger."

"How long will that be?" Jimmy asked dryly, knowing the answer already.

Roy opened the door to get out.

"It will be for as long as it takes, boy! You get that? Now sit here, both of you and keep quiet! Do you hear me?" he yelled.

"Yes." Jennie answered. The frightened little girl

lowered her eyes and fought back the tears.

"I didn't hear you!" Roy shrieked.

"We hear you good enough!" Jimmy replied, sarcastically.

A couple came out of Bessie's and gawked at the commotion.

"What you starin' at?" Roy snarled at them. Embarrassed, they hurried off to their car.

Roy slammed the pickup door, then glared at the children through the windshield for a few seconds before committing himself to Bessie's.

For a few miserable moments Jimmy and his little sister sat quietly and said nothing. Jimmy was nine years old. Jennie was six. What would they do? What could they do?

These four days alone with their stepfather had been terrifying! If their mother only knew!

Mary McCoy had made an unscheduled trip to Iowa. Aunt Viv had telephoned to say that Mary's brother Richard was seriously injured and might not live. Richard was always getting injured. He was a rodeo man. Staying on bucking horses and brahma bulls was the way he made his living. But this time he didn't stay on. Not only did the bull buck him off, it spun around and rammed a nine-inch horn through Richard's chest.

"When is our mother coming home?" Jenny whimpered.

"Don't cry, Jenny." Jimmy put his arm around his sister. "I heard Roy talking to Mom on the phone. She won't be back for a while. I know she asked to talk to us, but good ol' Roy lied. We were there all right, but he told her we weren't home."

"I wish I could talk to Mama. I'd tell her how drunk Roy gets and how he whips us hard, for nothing." Jenny told her brother. "Can't we call her in Iowa, Jimmy? I know she would come home if she knew what Roy was doing to us."

"We can't bother her, sis. Uncle Richard is dying. He might be dead for all we know."

"Can't we call Grandma, Jimmy? She'd come and get us. I know she would," Jenny pleaded.

"You know Grandpa just got out of the hospital. We can't bother her. She has more than she can handle taking care of Grandpa. He can't even walk by himself yet." Jimmy wished things were different.

Jenny whined as she snuggled closer to her brother.

"My leg is hurting again," she told him.

Jimmy looked at her. "Is that where Roy hit you with his belt?"

"No. It's where he burned me with his cigarette! He did it on purpose!" she cried. "Don't tell him I told you, Jimmy. He said if I told. he'd do it again."

"He burned you, Jenny?Why didn't you tell me?" Jimmy was furious. How he wished he were older.

He'd like to go in to Bessie's, pull Roy out of there and smack him hard for hurting his sister. How he wished he could!

"I was afraid to tell you," she said tearfully.

The children needed a good meal, and were getting colder all the time.

"We're gettin' outta here," Jimmy announced.

"And go call Mama?" Jenny asked.

"No, not yet. We'll have to hide somewhere for a while. Somewhere Roy can't find us. Button up good, Jenny, we're goin'."

Jimmy reached for the flashlight on the dash.

"Don't take that Jimmy! Roy will kill us!"

"Well, he's got to catch us first," Jimmy told his sister, as he poked a few more things from the glove box into his pockets and both their school backpacks.

Quickly, they scrambled out of the pickup and sped down the street. Thomas Creek was a small town. It didn't take them long to get out of sight. They headed east, out of town. The night wind stung their faces as they hurried along. A full moon lit their path.

Jimmy held tight to his little sister's hand and kept a sharp lookout behind them. They must not be discovered. Jimmy knew if they walked along the road they would be seen. When city sidewalks ran out, they walked in ditches, on banks, climbed over fences when they had to, and hid themselves behind

They headed east, out of town.

trees and bushes. Anything required of them to stay hidden from folks who passed by, they did. Luckily, there were very few who passed.

"We'll find a barn to sleep in along here. We'll be okay, Jenny. I used to go out with our Dad's Scout troop on colder nights than this." he assured his sister.

Jimmy knew he would soon have to get his little sister out of the cold. For the moment, no rain or snow was falling. But that could change at any time.

The sky was fairly clear; it was just plain cold and plenty slick underfoot.

They were about a half mile out of town and were about to cross a pasture to a thickly timbered area when Jimmy saw the red glow from the heat lamps in the farrowing barn. Ever so quietly they made their way over to the building and peeked in the office window. No one heard them, not even T.C. Papa was getting a can of pop out of the refrigerator. Then he sat down at the little desk.

Jenny pulled at her brother's sleeve. She was cold and frightened. Jimmy was cold too, but he was not afraid. Not yet, anyway.

"Let's go, Jimmy," Jenny whispered.

It took them a few minutes to cross the pasture and head into the woods. The trees hid the moon, making it difficult to see. The flashlight came in handy.

They walked along slowly in as straight a line as possible. Jimmy had no intention of getting them lost.

Then, there it was. The brave young man had found exactly what he had been seeking.

But could such a small boy protect his little sister from the cold?

The flashlight came in handy.

Chapter 8.

REPORTING THE ROBBERIES

It was Thursday, December 17. The phone in the farm house rang.

"Mom, these kids are driving me crazy. They're telling me they have all their Christmas shopping done, the presents are wrapped and under the tree, and now they're bugging me to bring them out." Deana sounded desperate.

"What about school?" Mama asked.

"There was none yesterday. The storm took the power out. They get out tomorrow for Christmas break. Mom, can you believe this? They've cleaned the house; not just their rooms but the whole house!" she laughed. "I guess they want to come pretty badly. How are the roads?"

"Icy spots, so be careful, ---but yes, bring them. We're ready, ---I think," Mama was just remembering how wild it got when all four of the grandchildren arrived.

Later that morning, Mama started to tell Papa about her phone call, but that was when he chose to tell her about the barn burglar.

The news did not go down easy.

"What? A week before Christmas, kids coming to visit and we've got a crook paying his nightly respects? Oh my! What next?"

"Well, I suppose I'd better call the sheriff's office and report this thing." Papa looked at his watch. "I'll wait until nine o'clock."

His day had begun early. At six o'clock he had driven his old pickup inside the big machine shed, down by the house, to load it with bales of clean, sweet smelling wheat straw. Before leaving the building, he glanced at the one and only hog pen there. The little pen brought back fond memories. Nice thoughts to warm his heart on such a cold December morning.

The pen had been built for Priscilla, Little Prissy's mother, the pig they had kept in the house. How he missed her. When spring came, he and Mama would visit her grave, back in the timber where Priscilla had been laid to rest. There would be wild flowers available then for her grave and also for Hotsie's, Mitzi's, and Mabel's.

"So many tears," Papa thought, as he wiped one

away that rolled slowly down his check. But now it was the living that must be cared for.

Each sow in the farrowing barn received a hefty armload of the straw. The sows used it for both bed and blanket. They were quite comfortable.

At one time, there were sixty sows in the long farrowing barn. However, Papa wasn't getting any younger and had cut back on the work. Now there were about two dozen. Next year there would be fewer. Only the best and the favorites would stay.

Even with the overhead heaters hissing and blowing full blast, doing the best they could, there were still a few cold spots in the barn. The outside thermometer read 17 degrees Fahrenheit. With a heat lamp in each creep, the baby pigs stayed as warm as a toad in a woolen blanket.

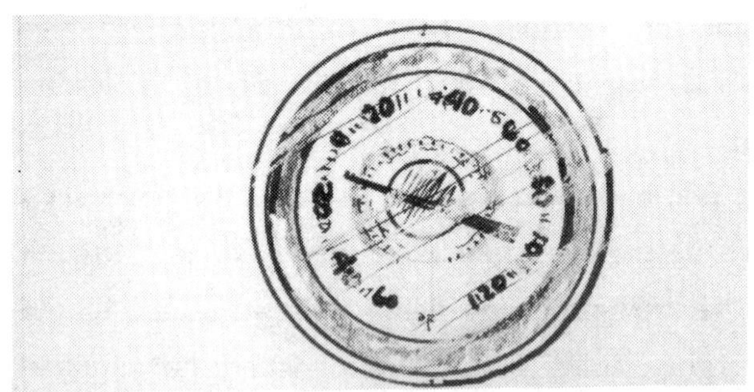

----17 degrees

Later, as planned, Papa phoned his friend, Sheriff Eli Thomas. Ordinarily, talking to Eli would have been used as an excuse to go into town, but with all the extra chores to do because of the cold, he'd have to make do with a phone call.

While Papa reported the prowler to Eli, Mama re-stocked the little refrigerator in the office.

Leeza slept peacefully on Papa's lap. During his conversation with Eli, he learned that no other rob-beries had been reported for the area. Leeza slept so quietly that Papa forgot about her. At one point, he straightened his legs in such a way that Leeza began to slide toward the floor. Suddenly, her eyes opened wide and she commenced to claw at Papa's blue jeans in an effort to stay aboard. By the look on Papa's face, Leeza's sharp nails had gotten through to the hide. He grabbed at the cat, returning her to his lap. A few seconds later the cat resumed her nap. It was Papa who first discovered the beautiful Leeza when T.C. brought her to the farm, and it always pleased him when she jumped on his lap at every opportun-ity.

Emily and Angel also napped lazily in the wood box. Slick lay sprawled on a feed sack, grooming. But John Henry and his father hung on every word in the office, curious to get the lowdown on this mysterious human who sneaked into their privacy, not once but several times. And, to think it had been done without them knowing. Both Tom Cat and John Henry were intimidated by that. Neither of them would admit it to the other. Stubborn? Yes. Pride? Probably.

Papa was off the phone.

Mama was anxious to hear. "What did Eli have to say, Dear?"

"He hasn't a clue! Said it sounded like the work of a local person, a neighbor, maybe. I can't believe that! I know all the neighbors. They aren't thieves." The neighbors were good neighbors as well as good friends. To distrust any one of them would be unthinkable. "Maybe it's someone who passes by here every night, a transient farm worker who didn't make it back south before cold weather. And, could be, somebody is playing a joke on us! But who? Who is the somebody?"

"It's no joke," Mama replied seriously. "People who know us would never take our blankets. They know about the chilly nights we spend out here in this old barn delivering baby pigs."

"Speaking of pigs, I've got to get started checking all the heat lamps. Can't have cold babies, can we, Leeza?" he said to the cat as he stood up and placed her on his chair.

Mama laughed. "You and those hogs! If those babies get cold they'll get in under the straw with their mothers." She was proud of Papa for being so particular with his animals.

"No one should ever be cold or hungry," he said.

But somebody was cold and hungry or he would not be stealing food and blankets from them, ---a fact they both realized. But who?

Mama searched the little room thoroughly. T.C. and John Henry made a nuisance of themselves. Both of them stuck close to Mama as she poked here and there. They crept along beside her and looked where she looked. A couple of times T.C. got right in the way. She gave the cat a little shove with her foot, but that did not discourage him. When no new clues were found, Mama bundled up against the cold and headed for the house.

But before she left, she moved a wooden box away from the wall. Although the box kept the cold air from coming in through the cat door, the cats would appreciate getting in and out on their own. Usually, on these nippy nights the cats got in under the heat lamps with the pigs. The sows were always glad for the company. They could always go to the house and were welcome to come in out of the cold, but they seemed to prefer the barn.

Emily and Angel began playing, chewing and biting on each other. Leeza jumped down from Papa's chair. Her foot struck a shiny blue object and sent it spinning to the center of the room. The girls watched for a moment before swiping at it playfully with soft, winter-furred paws. The cats had no way of knowing it was a little girl's bracelet.

Leeza looked surprised! She had never seen anything quite so pretty. But, where did it come from?

Chapter 9.

WHO DONE IT?

John Henry chose today to work on several of his "doings". Anyway, that's what he tried to make everyone believe. In truth, he was learning how to snoop. When two heads were together, he would get closer and listen. He didn't care if it was cats, hogs or humans, he just might gain some vital information toward solving the current mystery. So, he jumped about from one pen to another. Sometimes the distance was ten feet, a pretty hefty leap for a half-grown cat.

T.C. had always had a reputation of listening in on private conversations, but it was new to John Henry.

Once, Papa saw John Henry standing on his head outside Penny's pen. It startled Papa so much, he dropped his shovel. The thud frightened the cat so much that he fell to his side, "ker-plunk". Then he quickly sprang to his feet and raced out the door. But soon enough, back he came. All day long he hung around and snooped. All the while he listened, he stood on his head, or on one foot, or two. Once he even laid on his back and tossed a big round ball of dried horse manure in the air. This trick he did to annoy his perfectly clean brother. Once while Slick was watching, he got a little too close. John Henry slapped the manure ball hard with his right front paw. The smelly mass struck the poor, unsuspecting Slick right between the eyes. Slick ran off while John Henry rolled, as was his custom, with laughter.

Mama still had not told Papa that the grandkids were coming the next day. When she got to the barn, Papa was holding Patsy's little white pig, the one that looked like her grandmother, Mabel. Mama wished she'd brought the camera.

"Better be careful, you'll get attached to that pig," she said.

"Too late, I already am," Papa laughed.

"We'll never get out of the hog business if we keep saving back our favorites," Mama told him, while reaching for the pig.

Papa handed the wiggly baby to her. "Better be careful," he teased, "you'll get attached to that pig."

"You got that right," Mama admitted.

Today all the animals that were either nosy or curious were paying more attention. T.C. was above their heads in the rafters. John Henry was practically under Papa's feet. Do you suppose John Henry had washed his paws? Prissy and her daughter Pee Dee, Penny and Patsy were all tuned in to any news they could gather.

Had the heater not been directly overhead, neither Papa nor Mama would have stood in one spot outside the office for very long. Hogs require much less heat than humans.

While Mama stood there with the pig in her arms, she carried on a bit of a chat with Little Prissy. The hogs weren't too sure what they were doing, snooping around and listening, Little Prissy told Mama, but it was sort of fun. She also said that John Henry hadn't fooled her. Little Prissy knew he was playing detective, but he wasn't as clever yet as his father.

Papa was glad to hear that the grandkids would be arriving the next day.

"Do you think it's a good idea for the kids to be out here when we've got a thief sneaking around at night? He might try to get into the house."

Suddenly, something just dawned on Mama, ---a very important point.

"We don't even have locks on our doors. We've never had a key. This fellow could walk right in and slit our throats!"

"How do you know he is a 'he'? Could be this he is a 'she'!" Papa grinned. "Christmas is only a week away; maybe it's the 'Ghost of Christmas Past'."

At the mention of the word 'ghost', Pee Dee, who had her nose stuck through the 2x4's rubbernecking, drew back and stepped nearer to her mother.

"Don't be afraid, Pee Dee," Little Prissy grunted to her daughter.

Mama was somewhat annoyed at Papa's lack of concern.

"Ghost of Christmas, my foot! You aren't taking this thief very seriously."

Little Prissy turned her interest to Penny. Penny had called to her babies as she settled down upon the straw. It was feeding time. The pigs piled out of the creep, running over each other to get to their mother.

"I'm surprised Little Prissy hasn't given you a full report on our mystery guest." Papa loved to tease Mama about the conversations she carried on with her favorite sow. But he didn't doubt it for a moment that they understood each other, ---a bizarre fact that had come in mighty helpful over the years.

With hands on her hips, Mama faced Papa squarely.

"I've already asked her," she grinned. "Whoever the thief is, he manages to sneak in and out without waking anyone."

Papa shook his head. "Didn't think that was possible. Surely one of them saw or heard something."

Mama looked up to the spot where she knew T.C.

was perched. The cat stared back, consumed by curiosity. He had perfected the art of eavesdropping to such an extent that he was able to drink it in through his eyes, ears and every pore.

"Not even T.C. heard him," Mama announced.

The cat's nostrils flared. He was not amused! Already he was suffering a humungous blow to his ego, having to admit to himself that the thief had come and gone undetected. Now the farmer's wife was broadcasting his failure.

"Scrud! Usually, I get blamed for what I do," he thought. "Now, I'm getting blamed for what I should have done."

For Tom Cat the most humiliating part was to look foolish in front of John Henry. John Henry seemed to sense his father's feelings. He pretended not to hear by hopping around on one hind leg. Of course, all that did was bring more embarrassment to his father. No matter what he did, John Henry could never seem to please his pop.

"It's just odd for somebody to sneak in here without being noticed. A hog or two always grunts when we open the front barn door at night," Papa said. "Maybe they have gotten so used to us coming and going that they don't pay any attention."

"But you know how it is in the daytime when a stranger pops through the door. They all kick up a fuss," Mama replied.

Papa put a finger to his lips to shush Mama. He loved Christmas carols. The radio was on. Andy Williams was singing, "It's Beginning to Look a Lot Like Christmas." As soon as the carol ended another began, but Papa had work to do.

The tiny white pig was sound asleep in Mama's arms. Patsy called to her babies. Mama put the tiny one down so it could nurse.

Pee Dee was still thinking about the "Ghost of Christmas Past". Was there such a thing?

John Henry snooping.

Chapter. 10

GHOST HOGS

That evening, Tom Cat and Angel were in Prissy's pen when Papa and Mama arrived with sleeping bags and supplies. As soon as the two of them were out of sight and into the office, speculation among the animals began.

Angel had heard from Pee Dee about the Ghost of Christmas Past. Ghosts were another thing high on Angel's list of things to be afraid of. Pee Dee made matters worse by telling what Mama said, about everybody might get their throat slit open by this burglar. Pee Dee had turned her little head upward to see if Mama meant it about ghosts coming into the barn at night. She couldn't tell. She had studied Mama's face for an "is it really true", expression.

"It's so hard to tell with humans," Pee Dee told Angel.

Now, Pee Dee took a long, hard look at her

---two ghosts visited the farrowing barn regularly.

mother to see if she was bothered by the thought of the ghosts, although Pee Dee doubted it.

T.C. often told her ghost stories when she was younger. His stories always kept her awake at night.

He believed two ghosts visited the farrowing barn regularly. One was Priscilla, Prissy's mother. The other was Hotsie, who in life was Priscilla's best hog friend.

"Priscilla had two best friends," Tom cat was always quick to explain to Pee Dee, "Hotsie and me." For some reason he cherished the sow's friendship. He spoke with respect and affection about both sows.

Then his mood would change. His story was always the same. It never, ever changed. That's why Pee Dee believed the cat.

"They come here. They've been coming here to visit since they died. They look in on us. They told me so. I saw them both before the big storm, the night the burro got scared and kicked the barn apart, and injured poor old Mabel. They knew the storm was coming and told me to get home, I'd be needed, ----and they were right." Then the Tom Cat cast his eyes around and upward as if he truly expected to see them.

Each time Pee Dee heard the tale, she tried to imagine what the ghost sows looked like. Afterwards, sleep never came easily. Ghostly-looking images would creep into her dreams. But never, ever had she seen the ghost sows, nor was she sure she wanted to.

Once, Pee Dee asked her mother if Tom Cat's story was true.

"Yes. I believe it is," Little Prissy admitted to her surprised daughter. "When T.C. is just kidding, in the end he'll say that he's just kidding. The Tom Cat really believes he saw my mother and Hotsie. I have no reason to doubt him."

"Oh, mother!" Pee Dee had said in surprise! "What will they do to us?"

"Don't worry, honey. They will never harm you, nor frighten you by showing themselves to you,"

Prissy assured her. And how did Little Prissy know? She just did, that's all!

The cat family, except poor gullible Emily, hurried through the pet door to the office.

Slick had told Emily that a ghost was coming. He said this ghost cut off ears and poked out eyes from little girl cats, and hung them on the Christmas tree. Emily was now hiding somewhere.

Soon, the little woodbox was full of cats. The only time Slick and John Henry were nice to each other, was when they were in plain sight of their parents. Sometimes, they even wrestled around playfully on the floor. But eventually, one of them would get too rough. A fight would break out! But Leeza, good mother that she was, would box their ears for fighting.

Sometime in the night the cats moved to another location.

Papa and Mama slept in the office as planned. Since the stranger had taken their blankets, they brought sleeping bags to go on the cots.

Every animal in the farrowing barn had been alerted to listen for suspicious sounds.

Even though the sows planned on being dependable, only a few of them had their eyes open after nine o'clock. To these few, ordinary night sounds became suspicious sounds.

"What was that?" Only a mother sow calling to

Rain fell all night.

her pigs.

"Did you hear something?" ---Yes, but it's only someone getting a drink of water or snuggling in a little further under the straw bedding.

The frequent changing twangs on the roof gave rise to alarm. Rain fell all night. Sometimes loud, blown by the wind, sometimes soft, but always present. By morning, a severe drop in the temperature turned the rain once again into ice pellets.

Everyone was asleep, everyone. No one saw or heard the small images as they slipped quietly through the pet door, not Papa nor Mama. Neither of them awakened when the refrigerator door opened and closed. Quickly and silently the visitors came and went. They watched Mama and Papa asleep on their cots, wrapped up like Eskimos. The little figures smiled at each other as they silently and skillfully gathered up a few small items needed for their existence. From the light of the refrigerator, the older one spotted a local newspaper on the little table. He folded it ever so quietly and slipped it in his pocket.

Again they were gone. As silently as they entered, they departed.

By six o'clock Papa was up checking on his hogs. It took him longer than usual to get out of bed. Straightening up was a problem.

"My back didn't like that cot," he told Mama.

Neither of them was aware that again, the office had been pilfered.

The barn radio was set to come on at 7 A.M. and shut off at 7 P.M. This morning Johnny Cash introduced the day with a Christmas song about his youth in Dyess, Arkansas.

The only sign of Christmas in the barn was the large pine wreath on the office door and the endless sound of carols.

One year Christina and Sara had put a small tree

in the hallway, decking it out with lights and ornaments. It was gorgeous when they finished. But the barn cats got to it and all but destroyed it.

At that time, there were eight or ten cats hanging around the barn. Some of them were pretty wild, but nevertheless they were great mousers, all! The cats loved playing in the tree. They swung on the branches and swiped playfully at the ornaments until everything that had been half way up the tree, was on the floor.

Maggie, the old Springer Spaniel, finally put the tree out of commission. On that particular Christmas eve, the girls went with their grandfather to check on the hogs. There was nothing left on the tree except for the lights and a little string of tinsel. One end of the tinsil dangled loosly under the tree. Maggie grabbed it between her teeth and began to growl as she backed up. She was having a good time. Over went the tree! It looked sad as it lay there blinking quietly on the floor. When the tree fell, it scared the dog and she took off out the door. That was the last time a tree was put in the barn.

It was noon before anyone missed the food and the newspaper from the office. Papa went in to get his paper. When it was missing, he telephoned down to the house to ask Mama if she took it. She had not! Then he looked inside the refrigerator. Sure enough, food was missing. Papa wondered how that could possibly happen when they were right there not more than three feet from the refrigerator door.

When Angel and Pee Dee heard the news they became quite upset. Angel cried.

"It *is* a ghost!" Angel told her mother, through tears. *"That's why they couldn't see it, or hear it."*

The news of the latest invasion of the office spread around the barn like cold margarine on hot pancakes. Little Prissy's pen was the gathering place to talk it all over.

As far as Pee Dee was concerned, T.C. was the best authority on ghosts.

"Do ghosts eat people, T.C?" she asked.

"I can't say that they do and I can't say that they don't. All I can say is that I've never seen it happen!" he replied. The cat looked at Pee Dee, stood, and flexed his muscles. "Looks like it's time for me to take this situation in hand. Tonight I shall sleep with one eye open," he grinned.

"Huh? Nobody can do that!" Pee Dee told him.

Little Prissy had seen this cat do some mighty unusual things over the years.

"Could he really do it?" she wondered. "If he can, then perhaps by morning the mystery will be solved." Would T.C. discover the identity of the intruders?

Chapter 11.

FRIDAY, DECEMBER 18

Deana called in the afternoon. "The kids aren't gonna like it, but I've decided to wait until tomorrow morning to bring them out. If I come today after school it will be dark when I drive back. You know me. I don't want to drive on slick roads after dark."

Mama understood, but was anxious to see the kids. She told Deana about being burglarized again last night and wondering if the kids should come.

"These kids? Are you kidding? Mom, you know how they love a mystery. Sara reminded me that it was they who rescued Piston from old Rossi. I still can't believe they did it."

"Oh, I remember all right. How could I forget?" Mama laughed.

Mama knew the kids were as anxious to get out to the farm as she was to have them. Their delay made her sad. That afternoon the sun came out and cheered her a little.

The vet came to help Papa vaccinate some pigs. He also paid a visit to the big red barn. Victoria was happy for the company. Arthritis and old age had gotten to the old sow. Papa had fixed her a dry, heated area so she wouldn't be so miserable. Somehow, she seemed to understand that the shots for her arthritis were for her own good.

Papa couldn't bring himself to part with the old sow. She had given birth to eighteen litters of pigs in her thirteen and a half years, ---234 pigs in all. Victoria had retired. She had been put out to pasture, so to speak. Now she was pure pet, a pampered pet. She

would live out the remainder of her years as comfortable as the family could make her.

When the grandkids visited, each of them spent time with Victoria. They brushed her gently and oiled her coat. She would grunt all the while to thank them properly.

John Henry picked this day to roll, over and over. He didn't walk anywhere, he rolled. His fur was an absolute mess. His tail was a mass of frozen mud.

"Father, I rolled from the front to the back of the barn and back again," John Henry told the Tom Cat. Quite a distance! Very obviously the little tabby was proud of his accomplishment.

"Why did you do it, John Henry?" T.C. eyeballed his dirty son. "I don't understand you!"

"Well, that's for sure!" John Henry thought. "And you don't get a trophy for being a great father today, either!" the tabby told himself.

John Henry didn't care one whit if others disapproved of him, but when his father belittled his accomplishments, he was painfully unhappy.

Tom Cat watched as John Henry rolled away. "Where will it all lead?" He asked himself. "Why does he do these things?And, where does he get his ideas?"

T.C. remembered how sick John Henry had been from eating too many mice.

"Just wanted to see how much my stomach could hold, Pop!" the little guy had told his father happily.

But. when he got sick and the mice all came back up, he found out! Yuk!

Once the cat had stayed awake for two days and nights. He looked like a dead cat as he staggered around, running into things, fighting sleep. Finally, he fell asleep while standing on a grain barrel. Ker-wham! He landed on all fours when he hit the floor. Where he dropped, he slept! In fact, he slept all day and all night, setting another record without even knowing it.

Christmas was a week away. The presents were wrapped and under the tree and the carols were a reminder that this truly was the Christmas season, the season to be jolly. But at 5 P.M. the atmosphere around the barn seemed as somber as the overcast sky. It was a humbug mood. All was not well, not well for Papa and Mama and not well for the cats and hogs. After all, the animals' home had been invaded. It just didn't feel like Christmas.

Papa called the sheriff again, but the sheriff had more important crimes to attend to. He called Papa's problem one of "petty theft". Nevertheless, the mysterious visitor was causing sleepless nights and aggravation to one and all. It wasn't "petty" to Papa and Mama, nor to the animals.

Tom Cat had taken it upon himself to ask a lot of questions of the sows. He was sure someone had seen or heard something. Strange! No one had.

"Was it the ghosts of Priscilla and Hotsie?" he asked himself as he snooped around the outside of the barn. Any tracks he hoped to find would have been wiped out by the pelting rain and sleet. It was true that T.C. wanted to solve the mystery, but what he really wanted was to get even with Mama for blaming him. He had a motive.

"I'm not responsible for the hog barn. Even though *I am the brightest* of all the animals," he told himself. "Maybe she knows that! Maybe that's the reason she expects more of me!" When he realized that Mama had recognized his superior intelligence, he perked up a little. In fact, he liked the idea a lot. Telling himself so, made him feel much better.

Papa reached down and picked up Tom Cat just as he was ready to enter Little Prissy's pen.

"Are you heading for a heat lamp, fellow? If you are, you're pretty smart! " Of course, T.C. knew that already, but it was nice to know that Papa knew it too.

Mama was already in Prissy's pen. They were discussing Patsy's white baby and how much it looked Landrace, like Mabel. The Landrace is an extremely long breed of hogs, having large droopy ears. The ears aren't always handsome on a grown up hog, but on a baby pig, they are really cute.

Grinning at their conversation, Papa just stood there petting the cat. He could understand a little of

The Landrace is an extremely long breed of hogs.

Prissy's meaning, but not all.

"We won't be sleeping in the office tonight, Prissy," Mama confided. "If we can't catch this fellow when he's right under our nose, then we might as well be comfortable in our own bed." Actually, Mama and Papa had been right under the noses of the intruders and hadn't heard a thing.

"Not sleeping in that office sounds like a smart idea to me. You could be in great danger in there," Prissy told Mama.

Papa was thinking. "You know, anybody who is brave enough to drive on these bad roads, just to get a little something to eat, has to be pretty desperate. And if those two blankets are all he has for warmth in this cold miserable weather, he's in bad shape!"

To think someone might be cold and hungry was

not easy for Papa to accept.

John Henry had rolled right up to Papa's boots. All he had heard was the part about the burglar "being pretty desperate." T.C. heard it, too. Pee Dee was disturbed by it, of course. She crowded closer to her mother.

Would this be the night they'd find out just how desperate the thief was?

Chapter 12.

CHILDREN

"I thought you were all through out there for the day, Dear," Mama said as Papa bundled up again after supper. He put on his old plaid coat, the one with big pockets.

As he passed through the kitchen, he filled the pockets. The larger pockets were great for apples and bananas. Cookies fit in the smaller ones. There was a new box of Hershey bars in the corner cupboard. Like a little kid he looked to see if Mama was watching. She wasn't! Four candy bars fit nicely in his inside shirt pocket.

A cold wind stung his face as he rounded the house and headed out across the orchard. The rain had stopped for the moment. In his right hand was a long flashlight. As he walked through the orchard, he watched a car slowly passing by. "The roads are still icy," he thought. Whoever it was blew his horn when

Papa filled his pockets.

he saw the beam from Papa's flashlight. It had to be a neighbor, one who knew that Mama and Papa spend many hours in the farrowing barn at night. Although the hours are long and the work sometimes heavy, moments of pleasure make up for all that.

Papa unloaded his pockets onto the little table in the office. The cats wouldn't bother any of it. This stuff was not to their liking.

"Everything is okay in the barn," he reported to Mama when he returned to the house.

When morning came, Papa was happy to see that only half of the food was gone. The thief was not greedy.

Papa had not yet told Mama about the extra food. He could decide about that later. What would she say about helping someone who steals?

Actually, Papa only peeked in the office door to see if the food had been taken from the table. He saw all he wanted to see. Later, he would discover something interesting, a real clue!

Deana would arrive about 10:30 with the kids. By that time, the roads would be well-sanded and the sun was supposed to be out. There was plenty to do before they descended on the scene.

About eight o'clock Mama and Maggie, the old Springer Spaniel, checked into the barn. A blast of cold air blew them through the door. Maggie barked, announcing their arrival. Papa was putting clean straw in Rosie's pen. Heavy with the next litter, the little sow arose slowly to thank Papa properly. He rubbed her head before leaving the pen.

Maggie stood in the center of the little office and shook. Ice and wet chunks went flying all over the place. Mama turned her back, but it was too late. There were several messy bits on her glasses. She wiped them off before pouring two cups of hot chocolate.

John Henry and Papa came in to the office, side to side. Papa shivered a couple of times then moved quickly to the little electric heater, which whined a bit more noisily when he flipped it to high.

"John Henry, you look terrible," Mama said as she looked at the cat's matted coat.

"No wonder! Every time I saw him yesterday he was on his back, rollin' around, kinda crazy like." Papa told her.

Poor John Henry. He wouldn't have minded the criticism except that his father was in the wood box with the family. And, he was looking.

"Well phooey! Phooey on them all!" John Henry thought, as he went flying out the pet door.

There was a small scrap of paper on the table. Papa nearly set his cup on it, until he noticed something written on it. It looked like a child's handwriting.

Papa handed it to Mama.

"Children?" Mama asked. "This is a child's handwriting. It says 'we' that means more than one! How in the world? Where are they? What are we going to do Papa?"

"They don't take much food for there to be more than one," Papa answered thoughtfully. "Why haven't we seen them, and why don't they just knock on the door if they're hungry?"

What he didn't realize was that these hungry young visitors were just trying to get by the best they could without being seen.

The note changed things. The "thief" they had all feared was nothing more than some hungry children. And, they had said "thank you". Papa and Mama didn't want to see anyone cold and hungry, especially six days before Christmas.

Heavy, cold rain peppered loudly on the metal roof of the farrowing barn. Where was that promised sunshine?

"Did you ever see such a miserable winter?" Mama looked out the office window. "Where do you suppose those children came from and where do they stay during the day? They could be sick? I'll bet they are afraid! I wonder if somebody has hurt them?"

As soon as Tom Cat heard the news he rushed out the pet door to inform the sows. He loved being the first with news. So, the word traveled swiftly, this time like a three legged kid in a sack race!

Leeza and Angel were the only ones remaining in the wood box. The box sat near the little wood burning stove where a few hot coals glowed from the day before. Papa needed some small pieces of wood to get a fire going. To reach the kindling in the box, he held Leeza in his left hand while removing the wood from beneath her.

Leeza didn't bother with much of anything except caring for her four kittens. This lovely Angora was satisfied to leave all the worries to Tom Cat. She adored him. He was handsome and courageous, strong and clever. Hadn't he told her so? T.C. was definitely her safeguard and protector. Since the day they met, it had been so.

At the moment, Leeza's hero was enjoying himself. He had been on hand to learn that the mysterious throat-slashing thief was nothing more than some hungry, desperate children. Being first with news was a tremendous boon to his ego. In the next few days, he would learn that there is much more to the story.

John Henry watched his father as he visited hog pen after hog pen. He loved his father and enjoyed seeing him having such a good time.

"Look there!" Mama pointed to Papa's flashlight on a feed sack. It had been taken apart and the batteries were missing.

When Mama checked the frige, she discovered that a little more bread and cheese and two cans of pop were gone. Neither she nor Papa complained about the loss of the items.

"I'll bet there's two of them." Mama announced. "There were six cans of pop in here. They took two."

There was plenty of paper on Papa's desk. When the grandkids came they could write a note to the children. Maybe they would respond to another kid. The note would have to be written to be easily understood.

By nine A.M. the rain stopped. The clouds moved on toward California. A half hour later wecome sunshine laced the earth. Oh, how wonderful to see the sun. John Henry wanted to stare at it, but his father had to stop him.

"You'll go blind, son. This is one thing I will not allow you to do."

Slick hurried by smiling because of his brother's scolding. As soon as he smiled, he wished he hadn't.

"He'll get me before the day is over," Slick thought. For the rest of the day Slick kept a safe distance between himself and his brother.

Actually, John Henry wasn't concerning himself with Slick at all. He had something more important on his mind. It would be nice to find the children, but it would be nicer if his father was proud of him, because of it.

He had make up his mind. The cat saw it as a new "doing". He thought wonderful thoughts. He imagined himself walking up golden stairs to a golden chair on a large golden stage. He imagined his father standing there all dressed up in a white robe holding a golden crown. He imagined himself sitting down on the golden chair, while his father placed the golden crown upon his head. He imagined thousands of cats, watching and applauding, and, Slick bowing down to him. Ha! Ha! Ha!

"Tonight, I'll do it. The heavens will smile down upon me. And, so will my pop!"

Would John Henry become a hero and finally receive his father's approval?

John Henry and his golden crown.

Chapter 13.

GRANDKIDS

Maggie ran down the driveway, barking, announcing the arrival of Deana and the kids. The dog was happy knowing now she would have someone to romp around the farm with.

Papa came out of the big red barn and hurried toward the house to greet everybody. He had been with Victoria who was extremely uncomfortable. The sow had lost weight, quite a lot.

Twelve year old Shawn sat in the front seat with his mom. His older sisters, Christina and Sara, and younger brother Steven, were in back. The kids boiled out of the station wagon ladened with brightly wrapped packages to put under the Christmas tree.

"Take this one before I drop it, will you, Gram?" Steven asked his grandmother as she descended the back porch steps. He hugged a tiny bundle under his arm.

"It's for the dog," he grinned.

"Any new pigs, Gram?" Sara asked.

"Of course," Mama laughed. "Aren't there always? I have lots to tell you. Come on in. When you empty your arms and hang up your coats, come to the kitchen and sit down at the table. We'll have cookies and a pop and a talk."

"Golly, this sounds important," Christina told her mother.

"What's up, Mom?" Deana asked.

"I'll tell you when we are all together," she answered. "That way I won't have to tell it five times."

It took a few minutes for everyone to finish hugging, checking out the Christmas tree, admiring the decorations, petting the dog, and to settle down.

First, Mama told them about the food missing from the office and how puzzled they had been, unable to catch the thief. Then Papa told them about the note.

"We believe it's just some cold, hungry kids out there somewhere. Ours is the only place they can get a bite to eat. Anyway, that's the way it looks to us."

Immediately, the girls were ready to move into the barn and find out who the children were.

"Remember us, Grandpa?" Christina reminded Papa. "Remember how we rescued Piston from old Rossi? After an experience like that, sleuthing out a few kids will be a snap!"

Shawn had something else on his mind. "Steven, let's take advantage of the sunshine." On went their jackets and out they went!

The girls had planning to do to solve the mystery of the hungry children, but for the moment they wanted to get to the barn to "hello" the hogs. It was just something they always did. They began at the front of the farrowing barn and worked their way toward the back, "helloing" all the hogs, kissing the newborn pigs and petting the cats.

John Henry was asleep in the rafters above Little Prissy's pen. He was preparing for the operation he fully intended to carry out that night, alone.

Sara called to the cat but he would not open his eyes. Leeza and her lovely white daughters followed the girls around the barn. Sara picked up Emily.

"I wonder if Grandma would let me take you home with me, Emily? Maybe I'll put a big red ribbon around your neck and put you under the tree, for me."

"No way!" Emily meowed loudly. Quickly, she leaped from Sara's arms, clawed her way up a roof-supporting pole and did not stop running until she was high above Sara's reach. She was half hidden by the ceiling heater.

"Well, if you feel that way about it," ---Sara laughed. "I don't think Emily likes me, Christina."

"She doesn't want to leave this place," Christina

told her sister. "I never do, either. When I get here I always hate to leave. I love it."

Next, the girls went looking for Crackerbelle and Thunder, their favorite hogs. Just a few months ago, Sara carried Crackerbelle all over the farm. Thunder never liked being carried, but he took a liking to Christina and followed her all day long. It's hard to believe how quickly hogs grow up. Now, each hog weighed over 200 pounds.

"I'd like to see you carry Crackerbelle around now, Sara!" Christina teased her sister.

Victoria was pleased when the girls showed up for a visit. They felt sad when they saw her condition.

"Oh, Sara, look at this poor thing. She is so thin and she can hardly walk," Christina said as she reached for Victoria's brush. After some gentle brushing, the girls tried to coax the hog outside to the sunshine. Victoria loved the attention. She moved so slowly that it hurt the girls to watch her. As soon as they left to go visit Piston, Victoria went back inside the barn and laid down on her straw.

Shawn and Steven were already with the burro when the girls arrived. Steven was giggling at Piston who was busy scratching his hip on a fence post.

"Should we try to ride him?" Shawn asked. "He's well enough now. In fact, I think he looks really good."

"No! We are never going to get on this burro's

back!" Christina quickly informed her brother. "We are all too heavy, except for maybe Steven."

Steven looked at his sister, "Darling, (Christina and Steven always called each other Darling) I don't want to ride Piston, not ever. I just want to pet him or help Grandpa take care of him. Do you think I can give him some food?"

Sara reached down and picked up her little brother.

"Steven, this fellow is not hungry. I'm sure Grandpa fed him this morning, ---so when you see Grandpa you ask him if you can feed Piston this evening."

Steven hugged his sister.

"O.K.! I will," he smiled.

By the middle of the afternoon, the sun said good-bye and so did Deana. She wanted to get back to Salem before another storm moved in. By the time she'd rounded up the kids to give them each a hug, a cold gentle rain was falling.

"The roads are all sanded. I just want to get home before dark." she told Papa. Deana always wanted to get home before dark.

Papa and Mama planned to take the kids home for their Christmas eve. Everybody would open one gift, pig out on popcorn and fudge and sing carols. When it was bed time for the kids, their grandfather would read from the Bible about the birth of the

Christ child. Then Papa and Mama would head for the farm. It's the same every year, But, Christmas eve day was still a few days away.

Today, all four grandkids stayed outside for as long as the weather permitted. The boys helped their grandfather with the evening chores. Steven got to feed Piston. When it came time to feed Victoria, the boys wanted to make sure she got plenty, since she looked so puny.

Papa was proud of the boys. They were both concerned about Victoria.

"Let's give her more feed, Grandpa, and fatten her up," Shawn suggested.

"Maybe you boys can coax her to eat a little more. I'd like to see her eat like she used to. Poor old girl. She'll eat all she wants, and that's not much these days," Papa told his grandsons.

Mama and the girls were putting the finishing touches on supper. Christina had asked for ham and beans. In addition to that, a large green salad served as the centerpiece, looking very much like Christmas. It filled a big green bowl, encircled by fresh Oregon holly branches with bright red berries. Hot corn bread came out of the oven, just as they were ready to sit down to eat. Steven asked the blessing on the food.

The aroma from the table was tantalizing; the family was eager to get started. But Steven's prayer rambled on.

" ---bless Mom that she gets home safely, bless old Victoria and all the baby pigs and please bless those poor hungry children, ---the ones who have been stealing their dinner. In Jesus name, Amen!"

The prayer had struck a tender cord. It caused them to think about how really grateful they were to be sitting down to a good hot meal in a nice warm home.

Christina broke the silence, "Your table looks great, Grandma."

"Yes it does and pass the cornbread," Shawn laughed. Shawn had two loves, food and baseball cards, in that order.

"Did you think old Victoria needed a blessing, Steven?" Mama asked.

"She's awfully thin, Grandma. Doesn't she like her food anymore?" he asked.

Steven's question came from his genuine love and regard for the old sow. When any animal showed sign of discomfort, Steven became uneasy.

"Victoria is old, Steven. Her joints are all stiff and sore. The vet gives her shots and pills to help ease the pain," Papa answered. He, too, was worried about the sow.

"Look everybody," Sara pointed to the window. "It's snowing!" The boys ran to the window to get a better look.

"Goody," Steven shouted. "A snowman! I'll

build a big one tomorrow!"

"Snow?" Mama was concerned. "I wonder if those children will be able to get to the barn tonight?"

Look everybody, it's snowing!"

Chapter 14

GHOSTS

Christina and Sara had made plans to sleep in the barn. Knowing how they were looking forward to the adventure, Papa didn't like doing what he had to do. He waited, hoping the weather might improve, but it didn't.

"I'm sorry to have to tell you this, girls, but you can't stay out there on a night like this. Maybe by tomorrow night things will be different."

When the girls checked the good Christmas specials on the television for the evening, they weren't too unhappy about their grandfather's ruling.

"Well, I for one am glad you are staying in the house! I want some help with this jigsaw puzzle." When completed,the picture would measure 34"x 43". It was Coca Cola art and it included a foot tall, smiling faced Santa, drinking a Coke. Mama liked it because it was a bright, cheerful picture. It had lots of reds and was Christmasy looking. The puzzle was so large that Papa brought in a piece of plywood, cut to size. The pieces were glued to the board as they were put into place.

"I want this all put together and hanging on the library wall, by Christmas," Mama explained. "Don't you think it will look great with the red carpet and red and white striped curtains?"

Not caring a thing about carpets or curtains, the boys ignored her question. Shawn found a piece of the puzzle and applied glue to the back.

"I'll help you, Grandma." Steven picked up the bottle of glue.

"You'd better make sure a piece fits before you put glue on the back," Sara told her little brother.

"If it doesn't fit, I'll just hold it in my hand until it does, since I found it," Steven told his sister.

"The pieces aren't lost, Steven," Shawn said.

"The pieces are too lost! Why did you just say, 'I found one'! Steven had a point.

Shawn kept on working. "I'm just trying to tell you, Steven, if you glue pieces together and hold them in your hand, they'll get all stuck together."

"And I'll have a handful of glue, right?" Steven laughed.

"You got that right!" his brother agreed. "You'll learn; just start looking for pieces."

While everyone in the house was enjoying the evening, outside the snow continued to fall and to pile up. It was a cold, wet snow and stuck where it fell. Now and then the moon peeked through the clouds illuminating the blanket of white. Once, Steven looked out the window and gave a report. "It's daylight already and I haven't even been to bed yet."

John Henry loved the snow. He was overjoyed. The snow would be helpful for what he had planned, if it didn't get too deep.

About 9:30 P.M. everyone bundled up and went out with Papa to check on the hogs.

Mama prepared a small basket of food for the nightly visitors. Shawn carried an extra blanket. Sara located a couple of pairs of gloves, the stretching kind that fit all sizes.

Christina had been thinking about the note. She knew just what to say. In large letters she printed the following message.

"I hope that works," Papa remarked after reading the note.

The barn was still. The sows had settled in for the night. The grandkids walked along with Papa after specific instructions to keep quiet and not disturb the hogs.

Christina had trouble staying away from Patsy's white pig, the one that looked like Mabel.

"I just love that pig."

"Well, why shouldn't you? You're our granddaughter." Papa smiled and put his arm around Christina. She returned his smile. "You know how it is with Mama and me. We love them all!"

"But Grandpa, don't you think there is something special about that little pig?" she asked. "I don't know, I just feel kind of drawn to it. Isn't that silly?" she laughed.

"Name it, Christina, and you can claim it," Mama told her.

"Do you mean it? I have a name in mind already, but I thought you guys had come up with a name for her by now."

"Well, what's it name, honey?" Papa asked.

"Starlight."

"Why Starlight, Christina?" Sara asked. "I know you always have a reason for everything."

"You know we always say,

Starlight, starbright
First star I've seen tonight.

---well, when I got here this time, she was the first pig I noticed."

"I like it, Darling," Steven said.

"Me too! 'My' pig's name is Starlight," Christina wondered what it *was* about this tiny little pig. She had owned several pets already, but for some reason she felt she had never been given such a valued gift.

John Henry watched the family as they turned up their coat collars to keep out the falling snow and headed back to the house. Instead of bringing flashlights, tonight Papa had lit two old lanterns and handed them to the boys.

John Henry had slept all day. Tonight his eyes were open wide and he intended to keep them that way. He had scratched at a bale of straw in front of Prissy's pen until he had a little pile high enough to make a nice warm bed. Besides not sleeping all day, he had eaten very lightly. He had heard that too much food can make you drowsy. His plans did not include becoming drowsy.

John Henry knew that he and he alone could stay awake all night. After all, he had been in training since the day he was born. It was up to him to stay awake and watch for the intruders.

After a few hours of watching, the cat did find himself becoming a bit sleepy.

"Well, I'll fix that," he said to himself. "I'll do a few exercises."

What a sight. You could hardly call it a head stand. I guess you would call it a paw stand. Several weeks ago when he tried this, he had to brace himself against the barn. But no more. A little hop was all it took. And there he stood. Two front feet were on the floor and the other two were straight up in the air, --- tail switching back and forth for balance.What a sight, indeed! A couple of minutes standing in this position was enough to get the blood flowing. He was again wide awake. John Henry's "doings" were starting to pay off.

Suddenly, the cat was aware of a sliver of light on

The sliver of light grew wider.

the wood floor in front of where he lay. It grew wider. He heard nothing. The barn door began to open, slowly. The sliver of light grew wider. It was the moon, big and bright, casting light through the door. John Henry's attention was on the light beam. It was erie! He froze! Then something happened. A shadow began to fill the moonbeam. It grew larger until the shadow of a very big human filled the wide ray of light.

"It *is* a ghost," John Henry whispered. Frightened, he did not move a muscle.

As the door opened wider the beam of light broadened. Another shadowy silhouette threw its mark on the floor. Now, there were two!

"It's them!" John Henry was sure of it. *"It's the ghost hogs."* He crouched further down in the straw and kept watching. "They've changed themselves into humans." The little tabby began to tremble. He could not stop.

Suddenly, the shadows began to grow smaller. The door closed with a soft whish, barely noticed, and shut out the light.

For a split second a different kind of light flashed on the pet door of the office.

"Is it some kind of a flashlight? Do ghosts have flashlights?" he wondered.

John Henry strained his keen eyesight to the limit. The small night light in the barn was not very helpful.

"The ghost sows have great powers," he thought. "Not only can they change themselves into humans, but they are able to grow and to shrink."

Now, two small humans squeezed themselves through the pet door. Once they were inside the office, John Henry could not see them.

He mustered up all his courage. With rubbery legs, he stepped softly across the hallway and listened at the pet door. He heard whispers, human whispers.

"The ghost hogs have human voices," he thought. "How can that be?"

The pet entrance had a big rubber flap that hung down, serving as a door. The cat sucked in a long breath of air. He had to know. He had to peek in the office. Using his front paw, he pushed the rubber covering aside. A little light revealed again what he had seen, two mysterious small humans.

John Henry was afraid of getting caught. What would the ghosts do to him? What if they changed him into a person?

He watched while the two little visitors warmed themselves by the heater. Then one of them spoke, very clearly human talk.

"We'd better go. That man might come back to see about his hogs. He does that some times."

They set the basket of food, the blanket and gloves by the pet door. John Henry hurried back to his straw, wide awake and wondering what to do.

One of the figures backed out the pet door without making a sound. The other one poked all the stuff through the opening and then "it" too backed out the door.

Again, the kitten watched in awe as the little human figures grew into large ghostly creatures as their shadows grew tall in the moonlight. They had come suddenly and silently, and had left the same way.

John Henry had seen them. No one else had. What he wanted now, more than anything else was to jump right up and follow them. But his legs would not allow it. Fear rattled the cat and shut down the operation of his legs. For now, seeing them and knowing who they were, would have to be enough.

The little tabby's heart pounded. "I can't believe what I've seen! I must tell someone, but who? Not my father. He wouldn't believe me. I'll tell Prissy. After all, one of the ghost hogs is her mother. Oh my! What will she say?"

Had John Henry missed his chance to become a hero?

Chapter 15.

A SERIOUS TALK

Mama let the grandkids sleep while she helped Papa with the Sunday morning chores. She hoped for another note, but there was none. However, everything that was left out for the children was gone, even Christina's note.

The snow plow and sanding truck must have labored all night. Thanks to them, the roads were clear. Nobody wanted to miss Christmas services at church.

Little Prissy waited eagerly to talk to Mama. But when the time came to do it, she didn't know what to say. She wanted to think about it a little longer. Finally, when Papa and Mama were ready to leave the barn, Pee Dee called out.

"Mama!"

Mama turned and smiled at the sweet little face. Pee Dee was so glad Mama understood her. She had tried it before, unsuccessfully. This time she was triumphant. Pee Dee was so proud of her mother's ability to talk to Mama. She wanted to do it too and always made an effort to listen to them carefully.

"Go on, Papa. I'll catch up," Mama told him.

Prissy was not sure how to tell Mama. In great detail, John Henry had related to the little sow all he had seen, or supposed he had seen.

"There's something I must tell you. It's about my mother and Hotsie." She hesitated. "I want to think about it for a while longer. Will you come back later and talk to me, alone?"

Mama was taken totally by surprise. "Whatever is it, Prissy?"

Prissy did not answer.

"Alright," Mama said, stroking her head. "After church, I'll be back."

Little Prissy walked slowly to her straw. The telling of the story worried her.

On the way to church Mama was so quiet that the family began to wonder about her. Was she ill?

"No, there is nothing the matter with me. I was just thinking about something. Wasn't it nice that the food and other things were taken?"

"That sounds so funny," Shawn said.

Again Mama was quiet.

Steven broke the silence. "What I want to know is, what are swaddling clothes. That's what baby Jesus was wearing."

Christina laughed. "I looked that up in the dictionary once, Darling. Believe it or not, the dictionary said that swaddling clothes are strips of material that newborns were wrapped in."

"Well, I believe it," Steven replied. "He was born on Christmas, so they wrapped him up like a Christmas present!"

"Maybe, Darling," Christina smiled at her little brother while everyone silently chuckled at Steven's innocence.

On the way home, Papa made two stops. The first stop was Kentucky Colonel's. He came out with a big bucket of fried chicken hugged to his chest and a big smile on his face to match.

The second stop was at the drive-through at McDonald's for french fries and drinks.

Mama came prepared. She passed around small hand towels to keep the car's upholstery from being totally greased. She'd also brought a big plastic box to pass around for the disposing of the chicken bones.

Shawn was always happy when he was eating. "This is what I call living!" he managed to say between a bite of chicken and a handful of french fries.

"Are we going straight home, Grandpa?" Sara asked.

"Yes, I guess so. Mama says she has an appointment with Little Prissy."

"A private appointment," Mama announced.

"What's it all about, Gram?" Christina asked.

"Darned if I know, honey. She almost told me this morning, but she stopped short. She's so much like Priscilla."

An outsider hearing this conversation would not believe a word of it. But in this family, there was never any doubt about the words that passed between Mama and this little sow.

Mama sat there and thought about something else Little Prissy had told her, about the Tom Cat. Prissy said the cat had spent hours talking to the sows trying his best to come up with a clue about the thief. Mama remembered saying, 'for any person to come in the place without the Tom Cat's knowing was unheard of'. He was angry she had blamed him, but on the other hand, he sure would like to live up to her expectations of him. Telling T.C. he had not disappointed her, had to be done soon. Nobody else had seen anything, not even Mama and Papa the night they slept at the barn. She had not intended to hurt T.C.'s feelings. Now, since the intruders were believed to be children, the situation had changed dramatically.

Steven was anxious to get back to the farm to make a snowman. The early part of the afternoon was spent on doing just that. Papa came up with a brilliant idea.

"Roll those balls up the sidewalks and down the pathways, kids," Papa directed. If they did what he asked, shoveling snow would not be necessary. They did it!

Mama changed into some warm clothes and went to the barn, alone. Prissy was waiting.

"I want this to be a secret," Prissy told her. What a surprise! Mama wasn't aware that Little Prissy knew what a secret was.

Pee Dee slept. Mama sat down on Prissy's straw while the little sow spoke quietly and explained as best she could what John Henry had seen last night.

So, Tom Cat's story about the ghost sows was believed, even by Prissy. And because she believed T.C., she had no reason to doubt his son. The shadows of the children in the doorway had taken on ghostly patterns on the floor.

John Henry had described what he saw, or what he thought he saw. The little cat was terrified by the experience. John Henry was not accustomed to being afraid of anything, but this was different. For these reasons, Little Prissy believed the cat. Perhaps, just perhaps, she wanted to believe that Priscilla and Hotsie had returned, for Prissy had loved them both.

"My dear friend," Mama said to Prissy, stroking the sow's side, "it would be wonderful to bring them back, wonderful indeed, but, ---"

"You don't think it was they?" Prissy asked.

"No Prissy. They were not here. What John Henry saw was two little hungry children, and he saw their shadows change in length on the floor as they stood in the moonlight."

"It was children?"

"Yes, Prissy. Does that make you sad? Did you really want to believe it was the ghosts of your mother and Hotsie?" Mama questioned.

"I think so. But I'm glad now. I'm happy for John Henry that he made the discovery." Little Prissy's mood began to change. She was relieved, knowing the truth. "Well, I feel better now." she laughed, feeling a little silly. "I'll try to explain it to John Henry."

No sooner had she said his name than he came flying into the pen, meowing a mile a minute.

There is something he wants to show you, outside," Prissy translated for Mama.

John Henry skedaddled quickly and proudly to the outside of the barn. He stopped short in front of two perfect sets of small foot prints in the snow. Mama looked first at the tracks and then at the cat. She was thinking what a smart cat John Henry was, and he knew it. As Mama raised her head she followed the tracks with her eyes across the pasture. They vanished into the timber.

"Well, John Henry, you are a wonder! I've always known your father was a smart one. Now I know that you are too. I'll go get the rest of the family and we will go back to the timber and see if we can find some

Two perfect sets of small footprints in the snow.

kids." She petted the grateful kitten on the head. "Why don't you wait right here until I get back, cat. Maybe you'd like to go with us, huh? After all, it was you that discovered these tracks." The cat flexed his muscles and rubbed along Mama's legs.

Mama wasted no time in getting to the house. She was sure John Henry had a grin on his face. Quickly, the cat raced into the farrowing barn to share his news with Penny. His family was no where to be seen. As he passed by Little Prissy's pen, she called to him. The sow didn't want to see John Henry make a fool of himself by telling someone else about the "ghost sows". She'd straighten him out.

Mama was proud of John Henry. Would his father share that pride, or would T.C. be angry because it was John Henry, not he, who provided the clue which solved the mystery?

Chapter 16.

FOLLOWING THE FOOTPRINTS

Mama stepped lively across the snow, carrying her news. Four gigantic, pot bellied snow men welcomed her to the yard. One was wearing a bird's nest for a hat. One wore a basket. Two of them had broom handles stuck through their upper section, for arms. Beyond that, Mama lost interest.

"Kids, follow me! You'll be glad you did," Mama shouted toward the mass of snow people and grandkids.

Christina was the only one who paid any attention.

"What's up, Gram?" she asked.

"We're going to the timber. John Henry found tracks of the children," Mama was out of breath and excited.

"What? Are you serious?"

Papa sat at the dining room table opening junk mail. From the looks of the waste paper basket, he'd been busy.

"Come on, Dear. We're going to the timber. I've seen tracks!"

"What kind of tracks?" he asked.

"Children's tracks, in the snow,"

"Sure the grandkids didn't make them?" Papa wondered.

"I'm sure, and I'm gonna check it out. If you are interested, come on!"

She and Christina took off across the yard. Mama again called to the kids. And again, they didn't pay any attention to her.

"If they don't come, it's okay with me," Mama told Christina. "But I want to find out where those tracks go to before dark sets in."

Papa tried to catch up, but they had a head start on him. When they got around the corner of the barn where the tracks began, they paused.

John Henry was sitting there by "his" find, waiting. Now that he had had his talk with Prissy, he realized that his "ghost sows" were actually two little children.

"Well, I'm just a kitten," he told himself. "How was I to know?"

Papa caught up with them, and the three humans and one cat slid across the pasture. Mama explained how John Henry had stayed awake all night and had actually seen the children come and go. She didn't mention anything about the "ghost sows". That part could wait to be told when John Henry wasn't around.

"What are we going to do if we find them back here?" Christina asked. "If they see us coming, I'll bet they take off."

John Henry ran ahead.

"Let's try to find them before they see us," Papa suggested, not knowing exactly how to accomplish that feat. "We sure don't want to scare them off. Hard telling what we'll find."

"I guess we will play it by ear," Mama said. "We don't even know for sure if they're back here. Maybe they just walked across the pasture and went to the left or right, to a neighbors."

When they reached the timber, they lowered their voices. Not more than a hundred feet into the trees, Papa saw something.

"There." He pointed straight ahead, then put his finger to his lips. He stopped and spoke softly. "If I was a mind to camp down here, that's exactly the spot I would pick."

Smoke rose upward from a small campfire in under the branches of a giant Oregon pine. Lower branches spread to a diameter of more than 35 feet. The mammoth old pine had grown peculiarly. The

Giant Oregon pines.

base had formed itself into a small cave-like opening, a great shelter for anybody, adult or child. Under the tree, it was like being covered by a giant umbrella.

They saw no one, but could hear soft voices. Suddenly, the branches parted, and two surprised and frightened children emerged from the hideaway.

"Don't let us scare you, children," Mama said to them. "We just came to see about you."

The smallest, a wisp of a girl, wrapped her arms around the boy's waist. They stepped backward, ready to retreat into the tree's cave.

"My goodness!" Mama exclaimed. "These are

Mary Parker's children."

"Oh please ma'am, don't tell anybody you saw us," the boy begged.

With that, the boy had blurted out the truth, --the children were afraid of Roy McCoy, their stepfather, and had hid themselves back here in the trees.

Christina noticed how strangely clean they were for having been in the timber for several days. Their clothes were a little soiled, but they had clean hands and faces. She smiled at the children and took a couple of steps closer.

"You sure are brave to stay back here in the woods alone," she told them. "Did you build that for protection?" She pointed to a contraption made out of small poles and pine branches, and tied here and there with small lengths of string. It had served as a door to the tree cave. It was crude, but secure. "You really did a good job on that!" Christina took a few more steps nearer to inspect his makeshift project. "I'll bet you are a Cub Scout, and I'll bet you did this with very few tools."

"Jimmy took a bunch of stuff out of Roy's pick-up before we left. He'll beat us for sure," the little girl reported. The brother nudged her to keep quiet.

"Nobody is going to beat you, honey," Papa said to her. "We'll make sure of that. My wife tells me that you children belong to Mary Parker. I guess she's McCoy now. We heard about Roy leaving you out in the pickup on that cold night. I guess you're trying to keep out of his reach until your mother gets home. Am I right?

Jimmy felt he could trust this family. After all, hadn't they put out food and blankets for them? And that note! The note had even invited them to come to the house.

"If you knew who we were for sure, would you make us go home?" Jimmy asked.

"Certainly not!" Mama assured them. "It seems to me that you are a very resourceful young fellow, --- and I'm sure you could survive down here for a while longer, but it's warm in the house. You're welcome there. How about if we let you stay with us until we can get you back with your mother?"

As much as Jimmy wanted to accept, he hesitated.

"I'm Christina and these are my grandparents. Everybody calls them Mama and Papa except for me and my brothers and sister. My brothers and sister are up at the house making snow people. Now let's see. We know you are Jimmy, and what is your name?" Christina bent down and took the little girl by the hand.

"I'm Jenny. I'm six you know," she smiled at Christina. Christina picked her up and gave her a big hug. "What a brave six year old you are to spend nights back here in these woods."

"My brother took care of us. But the first night, we got cold." Remembering made her little body shiver. "Jimmy slipped and fell in the water."

Mill Creek was the back property line of the farm. From where the children were camped, the creek was about 200 feet away.

"My sister wanted a drink of water. It was our first night in the woods. I didn't know my way and the creek bank was icy. I fell in! The old creek was frozen over, but I still got pretty wet. I could have drowned." The boy began to relax now. He hoped that he and his sister were among friends.

"I was scared to stay in the tree by myself. But Jimmy made me stay there. He said he'd be right back. He wasn't gone long, but when he came back he was all wet and he didn't get me my drink of water."

"That's when I made the fire. I only had a few matches. So after I got the fire started I had to keep it going. My pants were about frozen to my bones before I could get my fire going," Jimmy grinned. "I put some rocks in the fire. When they got hot, I shoved a couple in the tree cave. They helped keep us warm."

"You kids are wonderful! Laughing about falling in the creek and your clothes freezing to your body," Mama laughed too.

"Come on, son," Papa patted Jimmy on the shoulder. Christina was still holding Jenny and Jenny

John Henry led the way to the house.

was almost asleep.

Jimmy looked at his campsight.

"We can come back later, Jimmy," Christina promised. "I want you to show my brothers and sister how you kids lived down here all by yourselves. I'll bet you have some interesting stories to tell."

Jimmy beamed at Christina's praise. She had the knack of making people feel good about themselves. He wasn't afraid of the family anymore, but he had many other worries. What would happen when his mother got home? Would Roy still be around? He wished with all his heart that his mother was still Mary Parker, that there was no Roy McCoy in their lives.

John Henry led the way to the house. He held his tail high in the air, but he wondered, "Has my pop heard about this yet?"

Chapter 17

NEW FRIENDS

There are no words to describe the "goings on" in the farm house that night. Jimmy and Jenny fit right in. While they were getting hot baths, the grandkids rummaged through their belongings for clean clothes to lend to their new friends. Jenny could made do with a pair of Steven's overalls and a flannel shirt until her own clothes were washed and dried. Steven had left some of his belongings in the pockets that were of no interest to a little girl. There was a lucky coin, a small padlock, four pop bottle lids that might come in handy as headlights on the little truck he was building, a length of kite string and the joker from a deck of cards.

Jimmy made do with clothes that had once been worn by Shawn and had been poked to the back of the guest room closet and forgotten. Not a perfect fit, but the kids were having such a good time, they did not care about size.

Christina and Sara washed Jenny's hair and set in some cute curls with the curling iron. Sara polished her finger nails. Christina found a ribbon for her hair, then stood her on a chair so she could see herself in the mirror. Jenny loved the attention.

"I guess I'm beautiful!" Jenny grinned.

"I guess you are," Sara agreed.

Soon both children were calling Mama and Papa, Grandma and Grandpa. It just seemed like the natural thing to do. And, it was beginning to feel a lot more like Christmas.

Supper consisted of hot vegetable soup, home-made and from the crock pot, with sandwiches and green salad.

"Hot food!" Jimmy exclaimed. He grinned at Mama and sniffed at the air.

How wonderful to have them in the house!

Papa slipped away to the barn to look in on his hogs and to think. His prayers had been answered. Papa was a tender hearted fellow. Knowing children were hungry and having to steal food had caused him some restless nights. He figured that tomorrow would be soon enough to have a serious talk with them about contacting their mother, since she did not know they were missing.

It was a calm evening; overhead clouds hung around.Warmer and dryer weather was in the forecast.

Papa hoped.

John Henry's news had spread full circle in the barn. The little tabby wanted to know what his father had to say about it. He'd ask Prissy. She'd know.

"Did my father think I was pretty dumb when I thought those kids were the ghost sows?"

Prissy studied the face of T.C.'s odd little son. "No, as a matter of fact, he didn't. I don't know how you managed to stay awake all night."

John Henry laughed. "I've had lots of practice! Then my father didn't make fun of me or laugh at me?" he asked.

Pee Dee listened. "Did you really think it was the ghost sows, John Henry?"

"Well, they could have been. I guess I was mistaken!" he answered. "There's no such thing as ghost sows. My father just made that up to scare everybody."

"No I didn't," came a voice from the rafters.

"Oh, no!" Pop was listening. John Henry was worried. He'd catch it for sure.

"Your father has always had a habit of listening in on private conversations." Prissy told the kitten.

John Henry was ready for whatever his father was about to dish out."Let's have it and get it over with," he told himself. He wrapped his tail around his body, ducked his head and looked around to see if anyone else was looking at them. Boy! Were they ever!

Strangely enough, the gawkers weren't wearing those critical glares on their faces that he had gotten used to. Some of them even looked pleasant. One smiled.

"Good grief! What's this?" the cat remarked.

"It's like Prissy said, Son," Tom Cat's reaction was most unfamiliar to the kitten.

"Is this a look of approval?" John Henry asked himself.

"This time, one of those 'doings' of yours came in handy. I'm proud of you, Son. You did something that the rest of us couldn't do. Not even me!" The Tom Cat's high regard for himself was no secret to anyone. But here he was, admitting that John Henry's "doings" were beyond his own ability. Perhaps it was because it was "his" son that he was able to say what he did. Whatever the reasoning, he had made John Henry happy. The day he had dreamed about had finally come.

"What? Do you mean it, Pop?" the surprised cat asked.

"Yes, I do. That was a very brave thing you did. No one knew for sure who was creeping in here at night." Tom Cat had to admit to himself that he, too, had thought it might be the ghosts of Priscilla and Hotsie. But he didn't want to say so out loud. "How did you manage to stay awake?" T.C. asked.

"When I got sleepy, I did this!" The happy little tabby jumped to his front feet. Ever so gracefully he

"When I got sleepy, I did this!"

lifted his body straight up in the air. His tail jerked from side to side , like a flag in the wind. To show off a little more, he raised his left front paw. There he stood on one foot, perfectly balanced. After a few seconds John Henry dropped back down to a normal position on all four feet.

Wanting to get a better look, Penny had stood with her front feet on the top boards of her pen.

"How graceful you are, my little friend. I wish I could do some of the fun things you do. I haven't thanked you yet for solving the mystery. Because of your special talent and courage the worry has been taken from us. Your father is right about your 'doings'. I always felt there must be some special reason why you did those things. And now they've come in real handy."

All John Henry ever wanted was the respect of his father. For now at least, he had it. He felt wonderful! His position in the barn had elevated. John Henry had an idea that this was just the beginning. He had reached his first plateau, so to speak.

"You haven't seen anything yet," John Henry told all his onlookers. "As I grow, I shall challenge myself to greater feats," He jumped to the top boards of Prissy's pen, flexed his muscles and talked his way to the front door.

"I shall run faster, jump higher, stay awake longer, stand on my head, one leg and maybe even one ear!" Just before he dived out the front door and was gone, he turned to his audience, bowed and grinned.

"Good heavens!" Prissy thought, "He *is* his father's son! That's exactly the way Tom Cat behaved, when he was younger!"

Now that he had approval, how far would he go?

Chapter 18

HAPPIER TIMES

Sara added an extra leaf to the kitchen table to accomodate seven plates. The three boys were still asleep on the floor in the living room, by the Christmas tree. Although there were plenty of beds in the farm house, the boys had begged to sleep there.

"Leave the tree lights on, Gram," Steven had ordered. "I want to watch them blink."

Sounds and echos of giggles had filled the house until after midnight.

"Shall I get them up or let them sleep?" Christina asked.

"Let them sleep," Papa answered. "I'm enjoying the peace and quiet."

Jenny was still asleep in the guest room. The girls had shared the big poster bed with her.

"I don't think she ever moved," Christina told her

grandmother. "The poor little thing was really worn out."

After the first shift of breakfast, Mama disappeared into the den. A few minutes later she returned wearing a jovial satisfied look.

"What's up, Gram?" Christina asked. "Are you hiding more presents in there?"

"No, honey. The presents are wrapped and under the tree, thank goodness. I just got off the phone with the Parker children's grandmother."

"You did?" Papa was surprised."You called her?"

"Yes I did. I figured she must be worried sick, but she wasn't."

Christina fired an angry look at her grandmother. "What? Doesn't she care anything about her own grandchildren?"

"That's not it. She didn't know where they were, but she knew they were all right."

"How did she know they were all right?" Papa was curious.

"Jimmy telephoned her from the farrowing barn," she laughed. "The first time he got near a phone, he called. He told her he and Jenny were okay, but they were going to stay out of Roy's sight until their mother got home. Jimmy was afraid to go to his grandparents' place for fear Roy would come there drunk and start trouble. She said, 'Jimmy is an exceptional young man. If he said they were safe, I believed him'. She hasn't told their mother a thing, --- said Mary has had enough problems. Anyway, Mary is due home tomorrow morning. So now that Mrs. Bowers knows where the children are, she said she will telephone Mary tonight. She thought it might be better to warn her before she gets here."

Mama took some meat out of the freezer to thaw. Then she remembered something else that Mrs. Bowers had told her. "Oh, I guess Bessie and her husband, down at Bessie's bar, ran Roy McCoy out of their place of business and won't allow him in there any more. But I'm sure he'll find someplace else to get drunk."

Something bothered Christina. "Why didn't Mary's parents go back to see about their son? Mary's brother *is* their son, isn't he?"

"Yes, of course. But Mr. Bowers had a hip operation a couple of weeks ago. So Mrs. Bowers had to stay home to take care of him." Mama answered.

Mama continued. "Mrs. Bowers told me that she would call the sheriff and let him know that the children are safe. Roy is in hot water over this. Wait until the sheriff finds out how he has abused these children. They're both bruised from the beatings he gave them."

"And Jenny has burn marks on her legs. She said Roy did it on purpose," Christina added.

Papa was slow to anger, but the thought of Jenny

being hurt was too much for him. "I'd like to ring that guys neck! I hope their mother has sense enough to get rid of him."

"What happens now?" Christina asked.

"We'll just keep the kids right here with us until we hear from Mrs. Bowers or Mary," she replied. "Probably tonight."

News travels fast in Thomas Creek. A reporter from the paper telephoned the sheriff's office to get the latest news of the children. Now that Sheriff Thomas knew the children were safe, he thought the community should be informed.

"Might stop folks from worrying," he told his deputy. "When a child is involved, it's amazing how the community gets involved too." He gave the reporter the whole story. About a half an hour later that same reporter and a photographer showed up at the farm.

When Sara told Jimmy and Jenny that their mother would be home tomorrow, they faced each other, held hands and jumped up and down and all around in a circle.It was wonderful to see them happy.

Feeling safe now, the children told their story to the newspaper. The abuse had begun as soon as their mother left town. In fact, Roy got drunk on the way home from the airport. When the children returned home from school, they got their first beating. Why? Roy had his head down on the kitchen table about half passed out. Jenny opened the refrigerator door

"Jimmy and Jenny were happy."

and woke Roy up. He flew into a drunken rage and whipped them both with his leather belt.

The photographer, Mike Straightarrow, was about the neatest Indian who ever walked in off the reservation. The kids all knew him and loved him. Mike volunteered his time in both the scouting program and Little League baseball. He and Jimmy were old friends.

"I want this picture to tell the community that you are safe now and happy. Okay?" he said as he maneuvered them around to get the pose he wanted.

Still, it was Christina and Sara who provided the right touch, when they placed Christmas packages in the children's hands.

"Are these ours?" Jenny asked. The children were

standing in front of the Christmas tree.

"They are yours." Mama smiled.

Jimmy and Jenny smiled, and at that moment the photographer got the picture he wanted. One that would definitely tell Thomas Creek that all was well.

"He is quite an exceptional nine year old," Papa told the reporter. "The way he took care of himself and his sister back in the woods on these cold nights was absolutely amazing."

"Mike told me that Jimmy is an experienced camper." He said when the children's father was alive he took them camping all the time. Jimmy got to go on several overnight trips. That's why he knew what he was doing in the woods. Yes, he is an amazing nine year old boy, ---thanks to his father."

After the newspaper people left, Jimmy became uneasy.

"Maybe it was a bad idea telling the newspaper," he said. "Now Roy will know where we are. He could make trouble."

"Jimmy, don't worry. You're safe here," Papa assured the lad. "With the sheriff and everybody knowing, Roy would have to be pretty dumb to show up out here."

"I don't know, he's a mean cuss," Jimmy answered.

Shawn tried to help. "Anyway, Jimmy, Grandpa has a good rifle and he knows how to use it."

Jimmy was not convinced, but he tried to put the matter out of his mind.

When the sun came out that day, the children all had mixed emotions. The welcomed warmth would quickly melt their snowpeople, but on the other hand, it would be a great day for exploring.

Sara, Shawn and Steven had not seen Jimmy's and Jenny's campsight.

"Great idea! Go for it, you guys," Christina helped the smaller ones bundle up and pushed them out the door. The old Springer Spaniel, Maggie, was hot on their heels. "I'd love to go with you, but I'll stay here and help Gram." she called to their backs.

As soon as they were out of hearing, she turned to her grandmother.

"Oh boy, Gram! Peace and quiet! Now we can get everything done in time to watch 'Christmas Carol' on television!" she laughed. "I love that old movie."

"We can if we hurry!" Mama replied.

But something happened that put a hold on all their plans. Jimmy ran in alone and out of breath.

"Roy drove by twice in just a few minutes time. What shall I do?"

"Go on back to the timber with the kids, honey. We'll handle it." Mama told him calmly. He took off running and Mama took down Papa's rifle.

What was Mama planning to do?

Chapter 19.

IT'S ROY McCOY

Christina looked out the window to see if anyone had turned into the driveway.

"What are we going to do, Gram, call the sheriff?"

"You go find your grandfather! Tell him about Roy!" Suddenly, Mama thought of something! "I don't even know what Roy McCoy looks like!"

Christina grabbed a jacket. She went flying out the door, yelling back over her shoulder.

"Don't shoot the wrong guy, Gram!"

Mama phoned a couple of neighbors and then Sheriff Thomas. The neighbors were closer and could get there quicker.

"Why didn't we keep Jimmy up here to identify his stepfather?" she asked herself. But the more she thought about it the more she believed her decision to send them to the woods was a better one. "Jimmy

There's a pickup parked out in the road!

was right to worry,'' she thought. "Here Roy is, and what is he up to?''

Christina had been to the barn and back. "There's a pickup parked out in the road just past the blackberry vines. Grandpa says it's him!''

Mama breathed a long sigh. "Probably is. Let's go take Grandpa his rifle.''

"Oh my gosh! Really?'' Christina couldn't believe what she was hearing from her grandmother.

The phone rang.

"Get it, Christina,'' Mama said. Then, across the orchard she flew with Papa's gun.

The caller was the sheriff. He was in his patrol car and on the way. From the sheriff came a description of Roy McCoy and his pickup. The man parked out front was definitely Roy McCoy. Christina had to run like a chicken thief to catch up with Mama.

Papa stood in the front of the barn keeping eyes on the pickup, which would move forward a few feet and then stop, then up a few feet more and stop.

"He's up to no good, Grandpa. What if he tries to make a run for the timber? Do you think he saw the kids go back there? I should be back there with them." Christina watched and prayed. So did Mama.

"This worries me. I'm afraid that jerk will make a run for the timber in that truck!" she said.

"How do you suppose he found out so quickly?" Papa asked. Then he answered his own question. "News travels fast in Thomas Creek, I guess."

Christina sat down on a bucket. She put her head in her hands.

"Oh my!" she said soberly. "I wish it was spring break and we were all at Disneyland." Suddenly, she jumped up and raced toward the woods.

"Christina!" Mama called after her. But she knew her granddaughter all too well. Christina had gone to warn the kids. It was useless to try to stop her.

When Christina was about half way across the pasture, with some 400 feet to go before reaching the woods, Roy McCoy revved up the engine, cut a sharp turn through the gate and sped toward Christina! He must have guessed her plan. After some 50 feet of graveled driveway, he'd be on the muddy, wet, winter pasture. Pointing the truck straight at Christina, he flew by the barn. Mama and Papa could do nothing to stop him.

Christina heard him coming and turned to look. Terrified, she ran faster than she had ever run in her life.

Mama began to cry. Papa lifted his rifle and aimed at a rear tire, but Christina was also in his sights. No way could he get off a clear, safe shot.

Suddenly, their luck changed. The pickup slowed up. The wheels began to spin. Roy McCoy's truck was sinking very fast in the mud. He was stuck!

Roy McCoy's truck was sinking fast.

Papa relaxed a little. "Gotta be pretty crazy to cut across a pasture in Oregon in the winter time," he chuckled.

Mama wiped her tears away and felt much better.

Bernie Lawson rode in on his golden Palomino, his hunting rifle strapped across his back.

"I'll check him out, Neighbor," he called out to Papa, and rode out to the sinking truck.

Sheriff Thomas arrived.

Christina was not in sight. She had vanished into the woods, where she would keep the children safely hidden.

The wet ground swallowed Roy's pickup like quick sand. By the time Bernie got to it, it was axle deep in mud.

Sheriff Thomas and Papa walked out, heading toward Roy.

"Roy told Mary's friend, April Thornton, that he had to get the kids back before Mary got there or she'd have his hide," Sheriff Thomas told Papa. "Mary will have to stand in line, because I'm going to put that man in my jail until we get this straightened out."

Papa was pleased. "Well, he sure left marks on those children, even burned that little girl, and she's such a tiny thing too!"

Roy was so busy inspecting the mired vehicle that he did not notice Papa and the sheriff until they were upon him.

He became a little rattled, "Now, Sheriff, I just came out here to get my kids. These folks took 'em and have been holdin' 'em aginst their will," Roy sputtered. "They kidnapped them!"

The sheriff looked at Papa and grinned. "Well,

Mr. McCoy, let me tell you something. In about half a minute I'm going to be holding you 'aginst' your will. Now put your hands behind your back."

It was a bewildered Roy McCoy who as he was being handcuffed, kept mumbling something about his pickup.

Bernie Lawson and Papa promised the sheriff they would use the tractor to pull the pickup to the office. There were a dozen neighbors milling around the barn with Mama by the time the sheriff placed Roy in the patrol car.

Back in the timber, Christina found the kids busily playing at the campsite, unaware of the events back at the barn.

"They don't need to see it," Christina thought. As inquisitive as she was, it was difficult not to know what was happening. Even Jimmy, who had seen Roy drive by, must have put it out of his mind. The children were delighted that Christina had joined them, and did not suspect that she was keeping them safely out of sight.

After a time, Christina peeked out to see if the coast was clear. All that was left was a muddy truck in the middle of the pasture. She laughed.

Later, when Papa saw the kids returning to the barn, he had an idea.

"They'll be hungry," he said. "Let's get them washed up and we'll go to town for hamburgers."

On the way to town Mama was worried. "Will Roy be back? Will the sheriff be able to keep him in jail?" She kept her thoughts to herself.

Jimmy and Jenny saw Roy's truck stuck in the pasture. Jimmy laughed until his sides hurt. It was a John Henry laugh. When he heard that Roy had been taken away in handcuffs, he laughed even harder.

"I wish I could have seen it!" he told his friends.

His little sister wasn't laughing about any of it. She was pretty frightened about the whole thing.

Would Roy return?

Chapter 20.

A RESTFUL AFTERNOON

The hamburger lunch was a great success. Papa and Mama beamed as the six children chatted between bites. After the morning's excitement, it was a pleasant relief for the whole family to spend the afternoon taking care of routine chores around the barn.

Steven slipped away from the others. He loved Victoria and knew she appreciated his visits. Ever so gently, he brushed her coat. The old sow was not doing well at all. Steven knew it. So, he talked and Victoria listened. Occasionally, she would give him a thank you grunt. He understood.

Papa had told Steven a long time ago that Victoria would never be sold. She was comfortable in the barn, but her arthritis was getting worse everyday. Her final resting place was marked out in the pet cemetery back in the woods. Steven had an idea that her funeral was not far away.

After supper that evening, the family gathered in the living room. Jimmy and Jenny were still there. Papa would take them to their grandmother's in a few minutes. Tomorrow was the big day. Mom was coming home. Her plane would arrive at 9:45 A.M., and Jimmy and Jenny would be at the airport to greet her.

While Mama and the girls made a neat bundle of Jimmy's and Jenny's freshly washed clothes, all ready to wear from their reunion with their mother, Papa gathered the other children around his chair and told them a funny story from his own childhood.

Even after Papa delivered the children into their grandmother's loving care, he was concerned.

Would everything turn out all right?

Chapter 21.

A FUNERAL

"I miss Jimmy and Jenny," Shawn said it for all of them as they ate breakfast. "We had a great time in the woods yesterday. Jimmy knows a lot more about camping than I do. He's nine and I'm twelve. Do you know he heated stones in his campfire and put them inside the cave of the tree? You'd be surprised how much heat they give off. He said when the stones began to cool off he'd kick them out and roll in hot ones. I hope it was all right for me to tell him to leave his campsight there, I mean the stones, the wind protector and stuff. We were hoping that Jimmy and his sister might come again sometime and spend a weekend when we are here."

"I'm glad you did that, Shawn, telling him to leave their campsight, I mean. And yes, the children can come to visit. I miss them too. I hope this mess won't ruin their Christmas."

Sara looked at the clock. "They'll be on their way to the airport by now, won't they, Gram?"

Mama's mouth was full of food, so she nodded yes.

Steven rubbed his stomach. "They sure are missing a good breakfast!"

"Yeah, they are," Shawn agreed as he stabbed three more giant pancakes onto his plate. "Gotta have some more of these to clean up all the syrup," he smiled.

"Sure, Shawn, sure!" Papa teased. "That was my excuse when I was your age!"

Christina stood up and banged on her orange juice glass with her fork. She had an announcement to make.

"Now listen, everybody. We've been so busy with all this Roy McCoy thing that we've forgotten to be excited about Christmas."

Sare got up and jumped up and down. "I'm excited! I'm excited!"

Sara was the family clown. It was normal behavior for Sara and everyone expected it.

"Oh, Sara, you know what I mean. I think we should really get into Christmas now. I have an idea."

"Here it comes!" Shawn pushed out a light hearted laugh between bites.

Christina paid no attention to her brother. "Sara, let's decorate the farrowing barn. Gram has lots more decorations and lights and stuff."

Mama stared at her granddaughter. "No tree, girls!" She remembered how the last barn tree was totally demolished by the cats and Maggie.

"Agreed. No tree." Christina remembered, too. "But is it okay if we do the rest?"

"Of course, with one stipulation! If you put up decorations, you must promise to take them down and put them away, right after Christmas."

"It's a deal. Not only will we put *them* away, we will take down *your* tree and all the decorations and put them away too," Christina's offer sounded great to Mama.

The girls dashed off to the attic for more trinkets and trimmings.

Papa had been outside for at least an hour. He came in the kitchen door looking as though he'd lost his best friend.

"What is it?" Mama asked.

"Where are the kids?" he asked quietly.

"The boys are watching television. The girls are in the attic."

"She's gone, Mama. Our old Victoria died peacefully in the night." His eyes well up with tears. Mama and Papa hugged each other.

That old grey apron Mama was wearing had wiped away a lot of tears. Once again, it came in handy. Tears of love, for Victoria.

"We'll have to take her back to the cemetery on the flat wagon. The tractor is still out of the shed. Bernie and I had a dickens of a time getting that pick-up out of the field. It sank more overnight. ---I'll have the boys help me dig a grave. It will be a muddy job."

"And a sad one," Mama said. "I've set aside a nice blanket to wrap her in. It's in the laundry room closet."

"She's lost so much weight, but she is still heavy. It will take all of us to load her onto the wagon," Papa said soberly.

When Steven heard the news, he cried more than the rest. "I loved that old sow," he blubbered. When Papa saw Steven's tears, he turned and left the house. He didn't fool anybody.

The little funeral took place in the pet cemetery, back in the timber. It was a tearful occasion. Victoria was buried next to Hotsie. There were four other large river rocks there to mark the graves of Priscilla, Hotsie, Mitzi and Mabel. Mama said a prayer. In it she said she was thankful that Victoria had been theirs to love and she asked God to please watch over the little resting place.

There were no flowers in bloom in December for the grave. The girls helped Mama make a beautiful Christmas wreath out of pine branches and holly leaves, with bright red berries. It was a lovely wreath. Steven placed it on Victoria's grave, where the river rock would soon be setting.

The suffering of her little brother was too much for Christina. She took him by the hand to lead him away. He kept looking back over his shoulder and crying. Christina knew how to console Steven. They'd talk for a bit about Victoria being out of her misery now, and then she'd take him to see Starlight and let him hold her. That would ease his sorrow.

It was the middle of the afternoon before things got back to any resemblance of normal. Steven didn't stop crying until Papa and Shawn set a large grey river rock in place to mark Victoria's burial place. Then he was satisfied.

The girls kept busy with their task of hanging lights and tinsil overhead and up and down the hallway. Occasionally, one of them stopped to pick up John Henry and pet him.

"How brave you are, John Henry." Christina hugged him tight. "I told Jimmy and Jenny all about you. They could hardly believe that a cat as young as you could be so talented and bright. Maybe when the newspaper hears the whole story, you'll have your picture in the paper. Wouldn't that be something?" The cat loved it. He'd always gotten attention, but not this kind. Now he was a hero, and the entire family bragged about what a special cat he really was.

Tom Cat bounced around from one pig pen to another. He even visited Piston and the feeder barn.

Tom Cat and Leeza talked it over.

Maybe he'd even visit the chickens. All the while, at every stop, he chattered his head off about what "his" son had done. It didn't matter to him if they'd already heard the story, he told it to them again. With each telling he added a little more to the story. He knew that they knew he was exaggerating, but he did not care. He was having fun. In fact, he couldn't remember ever having such a good time.

When T.C. and Leeza got together that day, they talked over another matter, and came to a decision. No one would be allowed to kill a mouse for Angel. No one! She must get over her fear of live mice.

"Don't go sneaking her mice!" he told John Henry. "She must learn for herself." T.C. and Leeza guarded the food put out by Papa and Mama so that Angel would be forced to hunt mice in order to eat. It was a difficult task.

The word was out. Angel was worried, and she was hungry.

Could she overcome her fear of mice?

Chapter 22.

CHRISTMAS

It was the morning before Christmas eve, and the weather was beautiful. Today the kids were to return to Salem to spend Christmas at home. As they all piled into the station wagon the local paper arrived. Mama read it on the way. On the front page she found what she was looking for. "Local Children Found Safe". The photograph was wonderful!

"Oh boy! Listen to this! Mary kicked Roy out!"

"Kicked him out? How could she? He's in jail," Papa was surprised!

"Well, he must have gotten a lawyer and got out. When he went home Mary had his bags packed, sitting on the front porch!"

The grandkids applauded the news.

"Did they put that in the paper?" Papa laughed.

"Not really," Mama grinned. "I talked to Mary's

mother this morning. The sheriff says that Roy will serve some time for abusing Mary's children," Mama continued.

Shawn offered an observation of his own. "I thought newspapers only printed bad news, but that was real good news."

Steven had a question. "What time will Santa Claus be in Salem tonight?"

Everybody waited for someone else to answer. Papa broke the silence.

"I don't know for sure, Steven, But let's see if the weather man is on the radio. Maybe he has seen something of Santa on the satellite."

Steven liked that idea.

On the rest of the way home the kids sang carols and talked about presents. Sara wanted a stereo, Christina wanted a new opera score, Shawn asked for a new bike although he had gotten a new one for his birthday in August. He didn't know what else to ask for. Steven's list was a mile long. Everybody had stopped paying attention before he was halfway through with his recital.

Supper at Deana's was pizza, a family tradition, one they all enjoyed. Steven went to bed early so that Santa would come. The rest of the family stayed up late and watched Christmas specials on television, snacking on popcorn and fudge.

Christmas morning was filled with the usual

excitement: the smiles, the thank yous and the hugs, and of course, the big mess on the floor. By 11:30, everyone piled into the station wagon and headed south, to the farm to continue the tradition. Christmas Eve at Deana's, Christmas Day at the farm.

Mama's table was decked out with red, white and green, except for the little pink pigs that held the napkins. They didn't match anything. The table was piled high with turkey and all the trimmings.

After the dishes were cleared away, it was time to attack the presents under the tree, but the girls had disappeared.

"I know where they are." Papa laughed, pointing outside, "they've gone to 'hello' the hogs."

"That's right,"Deana agreed,"even on Christmas."

"Especially on Christmas," Steven said, wishing they would hurry up.

Soon the floor looked just like the one they'd left at home in Salem. The presents were all opened with a certain amount of "oohs" and "aws", more hugs and thank yous, enough to last for a while. Steven got to open all the presents for the dog. Maggie wanted to trade, but Steven told her he had no use for a rubber bone.

As usual, Christmas day was wonderful.

Shortly after the last present was opened, the doorbell rang. There had been so much racket that no one had heard a car drive in.

Steven opened the door. There stood Mary McCoy, Jimmy and Jenny. Jenny ran in and hugged the girls.

"Roy's kicked out and he won't be back!" Jimmy announced happily.

Mary was a little embarrassed.

Jimmy carried a big basket of fruit and cheese, tied with a big red ribbon. He held it out to Mama.

"Merry Christmas, Grandma! This is for both of you. We want to pay you back for all the food we took out of the barn. And," he looked at his mother who had coached him ahead of time. "Jenny and I want to thank you for your kindness, the way you took us in and hid us and took care of us."

"Thank you Jimmy, but you didn't have to give us anything back. It isn't necessary. Papa and I were glad you finally let us help you," Mama said tearfully. Today, it was a red Christmas apron that wiped away a tear.

Mary was holding a large package. It was also for Mama.

"What's this?" Mama asked.

"It's from my mother. She made it," Mary said proudly.

Mama tore away the wrapping and could not believe her eyes. Browns, tans, rusts and gold, made up the most beautiful quilt Mama had ever seen. It was homemade and homestitched, the kind only loving

The most beautiful quilt Mama had ever seen.

hands can turn out.

"Oh Mary! I've never seen anything so lovely."

"My mother heard about the kids taking your blankets from the office." Now it was Mary McCoy who had tears in her eyes. "How can we ever thank you for your kindness to Jimmy and Jenny? They've been through so much." Mary watched her children as they talked with the grandkids about what they had received for Christmas. "Just looking at them now, I can see that they felt at home here. They call you Grandpa and Grandma."

Papa smiled at Mary. "Well, a person just can't

have too many grandchildren."

While Christina, Sara and Jenny dished up cherry pie and ice cream for dessert, Papa asked Mary where she ever met up with Roy McCoy.

"I married him too soon," she explained regretfully. "I met him at a ball game. We were both rooting for the same team. I didn't know he drank. We've only been married for three months, but that's enough for me. The children's father, Kenneth, was killed in a logging accident about a year and a half ago. He was so good to the kids. I was so lonesome, and Roy was available."

"And how is your brother?" Mama asked.

"Oh, he's tough. He'll be back on one of those wild bulls in no time. Richard has been injured so many times, but this time we really thought he was done for. The doctor said Richard's luck was holding out. The bull got him in the left side of his chest. We were sure he was going to die. But he had a good doctor. So, it looks like he will heal up and keep on doing what he loves to do." Mary smiled when she thought about her brother. "He's one great brother, even if he does have a crazy profession."

Then it was time for Mary and the children to leave. Jimmy and Jenny were invited to come again for a weekend while the kids were visiting. The grandkids were invited to the children's home.

"We'll see you soon," everyone was shouting as

Mary's car left the driveway.

Deana and the kids were in their car to go home when Christina said, "Wait. I have to tell Gram and Gramps something." She jumped out and ran to the step where Mama and Papa were waving goodbye.

"What, honey?" Papa asked.

"Christmas really began for us the night we carried that food and blankets and the note out to the barn for Jimmy and Jenny. We didn't even know who they were then. It didn't really matter, did it? We wanted to share. That's what Christmas is all about, right?"

Mama was proud of her. "That's right, Christina. Christmas never was just the 25th of December."

"Just thought I'd tell you that," she said, and off she went.

Deana's family hadn't been gone five minutes when Papa got up out of his chair and begin to pace the floor.

"It's too darned quiet in here," he said. "Let's go to the barn."

Arm in arm, Papa and Mama walked through the orchard. They talked about how life was never dull for them. A friendly neighbor drove by and blew his horn.

So many good memories from this old place. Victoria's burial had revived a few. Hogs? Who could believe they could be loved so much? Mama wondered if Victoria had gone on to where Priscilla and Hotsie and the others are.

Papa's thoughts were also about hogs. There would be fewer next year, and less work. The favorites would stay, ---and Starlight, so much like Mabel.

Angel ran ahead of them, into the barn. She held something tightly between her teeth. Could it really be a mouse? The kitten growled as if to say, "I caught it and it belongs to me."

Papa sighed as he looked into Rosie's pen. Rosie was in labor. "She's got four pigs already."

"And more on the way," Mama laughed. "Merry Christmas, Papa."

"Merry Christmas, indeed," Papa added, and watched another baby pig being born on Christmas day.

The End

(Turn page.)

Angel with her first catch.

How to order

If these items are not available in your local bookstore, you may purchase them by ordering directly from the publisher. Mail your order, with your check or money order to: Jordan Valley Heritage House, 43592 Hwy. 226, Stayton, Oregon 97383.

Children's books by Colene Copeland
(Ages 6 thru 11)

Priscilla (hc)	$9.95 plus $1.25 p&h per copy
Priscilla (pb)	$3.95 plus $1.00 p&h per copy
Little Prissy and T.C. (hc)	$9.95 plus $1.25 p&h per copy
Little Prissy and T.C. (pb)	$3.95 plus $1.00 p&h per copy
Piston and the Porkers (hc)	$9.95 plus $1.25 p&h per copy
Piston and the Porkers (pb)	$3.95 plus $1.00 p&h per copy
Mystery in the Farrowing Barn (hc)	$9.95 plus $1.25 p&h per copy
Mystery in the Farrowing Barn (pb)	$3.95 plus $1.25 p&h per copy

Priscilla poster 15 x 20, Priscilla says "Pig out on Books!"
$2.50 plus $1.00 p&h per copy

Priscilla Presentation -- Video tape (VHS or Beta) This is the author at school, telling her side of the Priscilla story, what it was really like raising a pig in the house. Kids love this hilarious tale!
$29.95 postage paid
rental -- $5.00 postage paid

Youth book by Christina M. McDade
(ages 10 thru 16)

Apples in the Sky (pb) $3.95 plus $1.00 p&h per copy

Thank you! Postage credit issued